Night Rumbles

Nancy Janes

Night Rumbles
Nancy Janes
Copyright© 2015 by Nancy Janes
jazele@live.com

Book cover design: Ronnel Porter
ISBN 978-0-692-31407-4
Library of Congress Control Number: 2015937912
Rockrose Press

For all who love the light

Table of Contents

Prologue

A research student in the astronomy department of a great learning institution created shock waves that rippled through three galaxies. His intent was not to interrupt the flow of life for any creature, but he did. And this is his story.

Brad, the nineteen-year-old student, in his fourth year of training in astrophysics, was a keen researcher with an avid curiosity. He had traveled extensively between galaxies since the age of ten. He loved his home and his studies, in that order.

The science academy was in the city of Iru, capital of the planet Lydo, which lies in the galaxy of Ourano in the third universe. Brad's research studies focused on the Netherworld's planet of Dluse, which intersected the human world in the first universe. The Supreme Lord governed all three existing universes.

On the fateful day, Brad was in the classroom to give a short presentation on universal behavioral patterns, a course requirement for his fourth year oral exams. He stood at the podium with Professor Mikol to present an update on his research.

"It's all yours Brad," the professor said. "We're waiting for your report on the Netherworld."

"A report on trivia, Professor Mikol. It's proving more difficult than I expected to obtain useful information on the inhabitants behavioral patterns. Their ruler known as the Head Honcho rebelled against our Supreme Lord in the far distant past. As a result, he and his followers were exiled to the Netherworld."

"Those facts are historic, and we all know them," said Professor Mikol with a slight smile.

"Yes, and my other facts, too." Brad replied. "Our inter- galactic journeys bypass the Netherworld. My plea to view the files of our Lydo security agents was granted, but no data on the daily habits of the residents is collected.

"Perhaps you can find more information if you take a field trip to Eyrl." Professor Mikol suggested.

"I did, but the reference Librarian said no current or past information existed on the social practices of the inhabitants. My trip to Eyrl's library ended in failure. However, there is one recourse remaining, Professor Mikol. Is a field trip to Dluse possible?"

"A risky venture rarely permitted, Brad. I will explore the possibility and get back to you.

During the next month, Professor Mikol consulted with the academic and government authorities on the possibility of inserting Brad into Dluse, capital and foremost planet, of the Netherworld. The most likely place was Nofer, a town in Daganland that intersected the human world. With the plan firmly set, Professor Mikol said, "It bears repeating, Brad. Your memory will be erased, and you will enter Daganland with no mind ties to your home.

In addition, you will take on the outer form of the natives who are mostly exiles from the human world. You are crossing into an unknown and dangerous country. Kindly Nofer residents may be in short supply. Are you sure of this journey to Dluse?"

"I will chance it and use the wits you think I have to navigate the darklands, Professor. I'm ready to go."

And so, Brad went into the darkness.

Three Months Later

1

Hitty, you'll never believe this," Brat said as he dashed into the room, and slammed the door behind him.

Hitty, sitting at a small table, looked at him with a frown, then stuffed her mouth full of bacon and eggs.

Brat scrunched into a chair on the opposite side of the table. "Give me some of your bacon and eggs, Hitty?"

"No, Brat. As you very well know, mooching will get you a fine of twenty pence. Your cup of tea the other night wasn't free. One pence is due. As I keep telling you, there's no sharing here."

"Mean o' Hitty," Brat said. "I don't have any pence to give you."

"Enough to buy food," Hitty said. "The dole is meager where scrip is concerned."

"And meager doles in everything else, if you ask me. These nights my scrip aspires to expand my brainpower not my stomach."

"Brainpower? Secret doings, Brat? Don't answer."

He reached across the tiny table and took a piece of bacon and a toast from her plate. "I won't Hitty. A cup of coffee?"

"Got none. Furthermore, quit slamming my door so hard, and fork over the two pence for repairs. I can't fathom why I ever nabbed you from Unis three months ago."

"My pence are lean for door repairs and food. Put it on my bill, I didn't ask you to nab me, did I? I can't even remember how I got here three months ago," Brat replied testily,"

"You piqued my curiosity as a foreign object, Hitty retorted. "You weren't the usual immigrant. But do go on with your spurt of news."

"The twins and I were assigned a case and we will have five nights to complete it. Swinne appointed Hassel and Vexy to be co-leaders of the project."

"Is that a reason to knock the hinges off my door?" Hitty said glowering at him.

"Me, oh my, you are the tops in Mentors," Brat replied. "Unis wouldn't glower at me like you do."

"You don't know Unis. Why are you so excited?"

"Because the project fits my research interest. Good luck came my way for once."

"Brat, recite after me; 'do not say the word good'. The word good is taboo. Anyhow, whenever Vexy supervises good luck takes a timeout and bad luck moves in."

"Then we'll have to toddle through the bog of bad luck together."

"Bog? An interpreter I'm not. Plain speaking is my style."

"Postpone your style jive. I want to tell you my story."

"Stop your lingo then and get to it."

"Lingo? Plain style? Oh well...we brainstormed the first night and came up with a plan. Then we called on the Earth- lings for two nights."

Hitty interrupted, "Humans are the proper word for them. I've never yet understood them. It's beyond me how they live like they do."

"Me too. Hassel sent us to a family of three who live in a house. They share lots of rooms."

"Can't compare to Daganland's five-storied buildings in the beehive design. Our own cozy staclet, too."

"Well said, Hitty. How they live like they do is beyond me."

"I said that already, Brat. But speaking about our staclets...our recent population explosion is likely to end in a smaller staclet for us if it keeps up. The Head Honcho keeps a gimlet eye on such."

"May his gimlet eye light on something else? My staclet is small enough as it is.

"Anyhow, Vexy said to us, 'Behavior mod strategies are to be used on the three humans. They can be willful if we don't press them to fall in line.

"Hassel said, 'Fifty-five percent of them do fall in line, twenty percent is iffy, and the other twenty-five percent is a big headache for HH."

"Brat, a coveted prize awaits if you can nudge an iffy into the fifty-five percent group."

"Don't go overboard with the prize bit yet."

"Overboard is tossed. Go on with your story."

"In a minute. Why are the humans so significant to us, Hitty?"

"Our world intersects their world. HH, Head Honcho to you and me, roams their land every night. Day too for all I know. The human world is a special interest of his."

"Why is that, Hitty?"

"In ages past humans invited him in and he's been in and out ever since, or so plays the sound track. Gossip to you and me. Info is sparse on the doings of HH. His policy is the less we know the better."

"To my story then. Once Vexy approved our plans, we slept the day away. Hassel stopped by at twilight with three tunics and explained the different time zones of the human world." He slid a round object from his arm and placed it on the table.

"What is it?"

"A gadget tuned to the differed time zones of the humans. It's a watch, Hassel said."

"What about the tunics?"

The tunics have a hoodie and render us invisible. We are to wear them whenever we have contact with humans.

It's a violation of the rules if they see us. Any lapse will net us a stint on the roads section."

"It will do that, Brat. Violations are easy to come by, so keep your hoodie on."

"It's fallen off once, Hitty."

"Watch what you say, Brat. It's a Mentor's duty to report an offense."

"That will be two of us laying bricks in the roads section. The first night we met I reckoned you were trustworthy."

"Oh, and what else did you reckon?" Hitty sighed and raised her hands in a gesture of defeat. "Go on with your story before we meander farther into subjects best left alone."

"Agreed, Hitty. The three Earthies were eating dinner and laughing with each other when we entered. I couldn't stand it, so I tipped the smaller one's glass of milk onto the table.

"'Dear, you mustn't be clumsy,'" the woman said, "'grab the dish dishtowel and do a cleanup.'"

"'But I didn't do anything,'" the young one said. The woman looked at him in surprise, "'Is someone else sitting in your chair, precious?'"

"The young one got up with a scowl on his face and cleaned the milk off the table.

He sat back down grumbling, "'I didn't tip the milk over.'"

"'Thank you love,'" the woman said, and leaned over and touched her lips to his face.

"'We must learn to be truthful,'" the man said to him in an indulgent tone.

"The young one looked at the man sideways with little daggers in his eyes but didn't say anything.

"I did feel glee when I saw the effect of my plan on the humans, but it disturbed me when the little one got mad. I haven't figured out why yet. Luna and Wim went into another room to canvass the layout while my campaign got underway."

"Imagine having to watch such doings. No wonder you were disturbed."

"You're right, Hitty, but what can we do?"

"You can do a scare act, but don't tell Vexy. The humans call us the Nitecraulers anyway."

"Never mind, Hitty. We're still the Silver Siders of Daganland.

"Back to my tale. I pestered the humans with little hair pulls. In between the pulls, they cast suspicious glances at each other. After dinner, they went to another room and almost plopped down on top of Wim and Luna.

"Luna said, "Ouch!" And she and Wim flew out the window.

"The woman sat beside the man and held his hand in hers. The young one looked at them hesitantly, then sat down close to the woman. The man picked up a small device and pushed a button. Suddenly pictures appeared on a screen-like contraption across the room.

They watched the images and put their faces together ever so often. "'My pretty dolly,'" the man said to the woman putting his lips on hers. "'My love,'" the woman said to the boy drawing him closer to her."

"You're a dogged sort, Brat. Me? I would have soared out the window and failed the course."

"You're not the soaring kind, Hitty. Don't go overboard on the flattery."

"I intend for you to get the point, Brat. Flattery is the number one tool used on the humans. A rule of HH."

"I get the point, Hitty. Luna and Wim did leave. As usual, I lied to Hassel and Vexy to cover for them?"

"You are not to do that. Offences, remember?"

Hitty said, leaning across the table to pinch his cheek.

He wiped his tearing eyes and said, "You're a scorcher, Hitty. You do spark me."

"Spark you? What if I flamed you into cinders. Wouldn't that be a sight to see?"

Brat's eyes widened in alarm, and he stared at her. Then he said, "Back to the Earthies. Luna and Wim did their disappearing act through the window while I took a seat next to the man and got comfortable.

The woman rose, went out, and brought in a big bowl of white fluff. They passed it back and forth with murmurs of "'Here sweetheart,'" I could barely restrain myself from soaring through the window like Wim and Luna."

"No wonder you felt that way. You were provoked aplenty. "

"Your Daggie sentiment heartens me, Hitty."

"Sentiment, Brat? Sentiments are not permitted."

"Not permitted? A future meeting on sentiments is logged, but to go on...

"The man sat with his arm around the woman's shoulders while the young one leaned against her. I poked him lightly in the side and he flew to his feet.

"'That's enough,'" he wailed, "'Dad hit me, Mom, and he spilt my milk on the table to get me in trouble.'"

"'What's the matter with you, Dad? What are you trying to do to me?'"

"By now tears were streaming down his face and he was yelling fit to beat the band."

"The woman sat there looking from one to the other, and pretty soon she turned a doubtful eye on the man. "'What are you doing to our son, Bertrand? I thought we had worked out the problem of your jealousy.'"

"'I didn't do anything to him. I swear I didn't darling,'" the man said.

"Darling then said to the young one, "'Where did he hit you, love,'"

"'He hit me in the side, that's what he did,'" Love said."

"'Let's be reasonable, love. Forget the pokey, come sit with me.'"

"Love sat down with a few sniffles and leaned against the woman again. It was going first-rate. The tears of the young one made me uneasy, but then the images on the screen attracted my attention.

"A scary creature walked into a house and a man met it with a thing dubbed a gun. When the terrified creature ran into the street, the man ran after it, blazing away.

"A gun, Brat?"

"A human device used to hurt one another."

"Can't use them here. HH sees to it. The rumor of his ample means to prompt obedience is freely circulated. As for you meekness is advised."

"Forget the advice, Hitty. Listen to my tale. I was so absorbed in the drama my hood fell off and brushed the man's ear. He stood up, rubbed his ear, and inspected the room from top to bottom. I darted behind the sofa and flipped my hood back on.

"The woman and the young one eyed the man with interest. "'Anything wrong sweetheart?'" Darling asked.

"'I don't think so, dear,'" Sweetheart replied, and sat down again. I was befuddled by this time. Why did they keep changing names? Sweetheart changed the pictures and stopped at one where a man was in front of a crowd.

"He was talking about something called love. I thought at first he was talking to the young one. Then he lowered his head while the crowd did too. He said, "'Let us pray,'" then he spoke of forgiveness and mercy.

"The man and woman bowed their heads and then said, amen. I thought a human named Amen had come into the room. When I didn't see anyone, my puzzle cogs wheeled their gears for a while.

"I watched the three humans while trying to decipher the meaning of what I had seen. Then the man got up and mentioned bedtime. He turned the pictures off and they went upstairs with me right behind them. The young one went into a room after more gushy face touching.

"The man and woman went into another room. A big bed, bigger than our staclet, was in the middle of the room. I hopped on it and began to doze off when the sound of running water interrupted my drowsy delights.

"I noticed an open door and went into a bathroom. The man and woman had gizmos in their mouth running back and forth on their teeth. They placed them on the sink, rubbed foamy junk on their faces, scrubbed a bit, and dried off with towels, like we do."

"Brat, there's interesting sights in the human world and you've chanced upon one. Their habits are much like ours in many respects. Since most of the Daggies are former Earthlings there's no mystery to it."

"I do wish we had a bathroom like theirs. A privy in the corner of our rooms? Heh! No gizmo for us. Plain sticks of a toothbrush."

"Better be content with our space and the toothbrushes, Brat. HH isn't big on the trimmings for us jailed birds."

"Content? I'll work on it. HH must hoard the trimmings for himself.

"Anyway, the Earthies took off the wrappings that covered their casings. Such weird looking beings. Long and lean forms like a cylinder and knobby limbs with projecting tentacles on the end of them."

"Not everyone can be beautiful, like us, Brat, with our pretty little feet with three toes, and hands with three fingers. Humans don't have tentacles. They have five toes on each foot and five fingers on each hand. The casings are their bodies. Names for them are humans, Homo sapiens, Earthlings, man, woman, boy and girl. You met a boy produced by the woman and man."

"Whatever, Hitty. How did the two humans produce a boy? Do you know?"

"Read a book on human physiology, Brat."

"When time allows, Hitty. To my story now.

They put on fresh wrappings and lay down on the bed. "'Darling,' the man said in a whisper, 'did you sense a malicious presence lurking near us this evening. I thought for a moment I glimpsed shifty eyes in a red mist.'"

"'Sweetheart, something is happening but I don't know what. Let us watch and pray,'" the woman replied.

"My mouth flew open. I shot out the door and went into the young one's room. He slept so peacefully I was tempted to lie down beside him, but my studies called me home."

"A good move, Brat. Don't tell Vexy your hood fell off. She and Hassel gave you an advanced case. May be one from the twenty-five percent."

"I thought I'd skip the case tonight, Hitty. The humans might twig to my game. We have two more nights anyhow. I'm still mad at the man for saying I was malicious and shifty eyed."

"Cool it, Brat. Don't ruin your corporate career. The shovel brigade at The Works is brimful with hotheads."

"Luna and Wim will end up there if they don't mind themselves. I saw Vexy's horrid smile when she handed us the assignment. She's the honer, and we're the whetstone. She's so rattler-like."

"Right you are, Brat. She and I have had a few tussles in our time, and the winner wasn't me. So keep your shifty eyes open."

"Shifty eyes? There you go, Hitty. That's a tweezer from you."

"It's more a compliment, Brat. We do have shifty eyes. It comes from being servile when we step outside our staclets. And between you and me, being malicious is the name of the game."

"I never thought of that, Hitty. So much to notice." "Your noggin' is for thinking, Brat, and notice is recommended. Keep two steps ahead of your masters but lower your head in their presence."

"Advice is not to be ignored. I'll think on it, Hitty. It's bedtime for me, I'm beat. Wim and Luna are coming by before class tomorrow night. I'll clue them in to their fate if they don't take care."

"They're playing a dicey game. Don't fall into the coal pits with them," she said as he went through the door and slammed it behind him.

A restless sleep during the day and a session with his teammates at nightfall added to his moodiness. "You're too much Brat," Luna said, then she giggled when he tried to warn them about Vexy. "We don't mind her a bit. Our case notes are faked."

"I've warned you." Brat replied. "Hitty has been around the track and knows from the get-go."

He gathered up his class materials and they walked the short distance to the educational building.

"Our novice and my ace trainees," Vexy said, as they entered the room. She and Hassel looked at them with slanted eyes and grinned with every pointy tooth showing.

"Your reports. Begin Brat," Vexy said. He described his observations and said, "Vexy, the humans are certainly a puzzle. Maybe you can explain their actions to me."

"Hold on, Brat, until the case is closed." Hassel said. He sat down on Brat's right, and gave him another toothy grin.

"Now you two," Vexy said to Luna and Wim. Each took turns reading their notes, then they added a story of the Earthlings were outwitted.

"As I expected," Vexy said.

She looked at Brat. "You did the proper thing in postponing your visit. We don't want to frighten the three humans. Tonight you will start researching another trio of them. A chief executive, an investment banker and a politician. You can add an extra to the group or remove one.

"Wim, you and Luna will undertake a study on mineral resources and their use in our country. A key assignment, so don't neglect it." She gazed at them with stern eyes from her vixen's face and smiled sweetly. "My stars," she said. "Do well and I'll guarantee your reward."

On dismissal, Hassel said, "We will meet in the classroom for the rest of the term. The books for your studies are in the library. Check them out as necessary."

"See, Brat, what a pushover she is," Wim said on their way home. "Look what a compliment she paid us by the major assignment."

"Maybe, but you and Luna watch yourselves. Minerals are a basic vocation here. My tip is to cram lessons into your fun loving heads."

The night was far advanced by the time Brat had completed his studies. He noted the main points then slept throughout the day and got up at twilight. After showering and dressing, he ate his meager meal and said to himself, *I like the humans. This task is a go-go for me.*

On entering the house of the humans, he was astonished to see a group sitting in a circle. "Whoa! What's that light? And who are all these other Earthies?" he spoke aloud.

Wim and Luna came in from another room. "Look at the spineless humans," Wim said. "They brought in the big guns because they were shaking on their feets."

A light with sword like rays enveloped the people who sat in the living room with lowered heads.

"They're on to us," Wim said, "and doing the amen thing. No use to stay."

"Vexy can't blame us; she and Hassel sent us to the humans." Luna said. "Might as well tell her now. Are you with us, Brat?"

"Vexy, the case fell apart," Wim said in an excited tone of voice as they entered the classroom.

Vexy, surprised by their early arrival, looked at Wim with narrowed crimson eyes. "Oh, did it, Wim? And do you have your case notes?"

"No, we came straight here from the Earthies."

"And you have yours, Brat."

"On tape," he replied, showing her the small recorder for student use.

"Jot your notes down and give them to me in fifteen minutes," she said with a scowl.

They sat and composed their reports and handed them to her. She read their notes, then looked intently at them.

"Stay a minute, Brat," she said, and dismissed Luna and Wim with a curt nod.

"You have carried out your assignment as ordered," she said after closing the door behind them.

"How about Luna and Wim?" he asked.

"Never mind about them. You do as you are told. I have the very thing for them after they finish the mineral resource assignment.

"Research the trio of humans, their profession, and behavior, then write your report. You can begin direct observations, if you wish, along with your research." She picked up a hefty book and handed it to him, "A history on the manners and customs of the humans. An invaluable resource."

"The humans didn't hear me when I spoke out loud. Why is that, Vexy?"

"We are on a different tonal circuit, but if you get close they can hear you."

"Thanks, I'll keep my distance. Is Hassel okay?"

"No concern of yours. Hassel may be on leave for some time, but I'm here for you."

Radical Leanings

2

Hitty, wait until I tell you this," Brat said as he slammed the door behind him.

"Brat, I'm going to slam you one if you keep slamming my door," Hitty snapped.

"Sorry. The news running amok in my head is sprinting at such a pace; I can't remember anything you say to me.

"Guess what. Our assignment to the three Earthies ended in failure. Vexy gave me a new assignment on the humans. Luna and Wim will share theirs on mineral resources.

"Hassel wasn't in class, but you know, Hitty, of the two of them, he's the best instructor. Vexy bullies him."

"That's how it is, Brat. The feminine principle at work, HH says. Bullying or no bullying, Hassel will suffer when trouble comes hoofing, and where Vexy is, trouble hoofs right along with her.

"Right now, Brat, rules are in order. I'm your Mentor. No more banging my door. You ran off without paying for your bacon and toast. No more of that either. You hear me."

"I hear you, Hitty," he said and crossed six fingers behind his back. "Could we have an omelet to seal our treaty?"

"You do beat all, Brat. I'll make us a bit, but pay first. I have coffee and bread for you."

"Can I help it if HH okayed our eating? I'm taking advantage of what's available."

"If you can pay for them. It's pay on demand here. Eats are the one thing we can do without penalty. Give credit to the humans for the perk."

"Credit, Hitty?"

"Meaning humans need to eat even in this place."

"A poor frill it is. Nothing but eats, and that in short supply. Sleep and work, no friends, no social outings, no parks, no public anything," Brat said. "The human world is much better than our world. I envy them."

"You're a right smart Daggie, so keep your mouth zipped, and eat your food. Count your thanks. We get one public outing. The Head Honcho runs through town to let us know who's boss. We sneak around corners to see a friend and share a tea with each other."

She tallied up the coins he gave her and put them into the bowl on the counter. "Don't go near the bowl, Brat. I know what you do when I'm not looking."

"I won't, Hitty. A glass of OJ sets off an omelet. Do you have a pat of real butter for my toast?"

"Never mind, Brat. Go get OJ and the butter too if you're panting for them."

"Next time. Buy a little jam, please. Right now I need answers to these burning questions about the Earthies."

"Burning, Brat?"

"Don't start that, Hitty. You know what I mean. And since we're on the subject, I might as well tell you, I don't like your nips. I want you to stop them, and wipe the ridiculous smirk off your face."

"I'm only trying to toughen you up, Brat. If you don't grow into a loutish oaf, you won't make it. You'll be on a job sector one step lower than the shovel brigade. What's more I'll be there with you."

"Lay off me for a while and we'll revisit the subject. If my thuggy qualities aren't growing, you can redouble the louts."

"I'll lay off, but I warn you our super-stars aren't the understanding type. As I said before, no benefactors live in these parts. No psychiatrists either. However, you'll find lots of them on the Roads Project, and that's the chore for you if you fail to shape up.

"The RGI is always on the repair schedule, a toll road, heavily traveled twenty-four hours a night. You make your own bricks hot from the ovens. To and fro you go. The big brass whizz by ever so often to pounce on loafers."

"I hear you, Hitty. My ears are open to the beguiling attractions of our politics. I'm on watch and aspire to a few of the ploys of our Big Boss. By the way, what is the RGI?"

"The RGI is the road of good intentions. The road connects Daganland and the human world. We are forbidden its use. About your fiery questions? Still on fire to get your answers?"

"Let me stir the ashes up. You do dampen me down to flickers."

"Flicker up to an inferno, Brat, I'm listening. Your eats will be torched while we talk."

He related the details of the visit made earlier in the evening and the meeting with Vexy later.

"I want to know why the humans were sitting within a ring of light. Also, why couldn't we get close to the light? I could barely see it was so bright."

"The ones you visited are in the twenty-five percent category. The biggest Honcho of all protects them. Our Chief Honcho isn't in his league, but he muscles in at every opportunity. One ploy he uses is to sic the brainy psychological types on the human world and woo them to Dluse."

"If there's a bigger Honcho how come we're here and not there?"

"How should I know, Brat? If I knew, I wouldn't be here. No use asking such a question. Expend your energy on navigating these districts."

"In that case, why did Vexy and Hassel send us to three humans in the twenty-five percent category?"

She put two plates of food on the table, poured two cups of coffee, then sat down at the table. "My guess is Vexy was testing Luna and Wim. She employs spies, sets her traps, and patiently waits before taking her proof to the evidentiary bureau."

"How did I get into the case?"

"You were caught in her setup. Don't take it personally. Vexy uses whoever is in her sight at the moment."

"I'll remember that bit of info, Hitty. Might come in handy some night."

"You never can tell, Brat. As to the why of the light? I've heard prattle that the Supreme Chief has warriors that come to the defense of the twenty five percent. The light is a reflection from the beings he sends to protect them."

"No one comes to help us, Hitty. Why is that?"

"Our Head Honcho doesn't believe in helping, Brat. That's why. "

"I'll have to think on that and get back to you on the subject."

"You do that. Much good your thinking will do."

"I'd like more than anything to meet the Supreme Chief of the Earthlings."

"No more of that talk, Brat," she said with her eyes rounded and her mouth opened in a horrified look. "A ten year sentence in the Gulag if there's a whisper of the Supreme Chief. It's down on the seventh floor and a hold for many Daggies who venture to disobey the rules of HH."

"I'll avoid the Gulag, Hitty. Steering me through the perils of Vexy and Hassel is enough. Can't you even give me an inkling of where the Supreme Chief lives?"

"All I know, Brat, is that he rules from Ourano the galaxy in the third universe. The buzz is he rules all three universes. We don't even know what galaxy we're in, but we're in the first universe. Now tell me about your new assignment."

"First... Ourano and the third universe? Where are they located?"

"Don't vex me with your questions, Brat, I'm not an astronomer. The planet Lydo is in it because HH spews his fury towards it periodically. Otherwise we wouldn't know its name."

Brat sighed, pursed his lips, and said, "Realities then...Vexy gave me a research project on the humans. I have to learn their customs and speech patterns, and to top it off, I have to observe a trio of them. The first is a chief executive officer."

"Well, Brat, there are many CEO's paving on the RGI and shoveling coal at The Works. An interview with one might prove helpful."

"She wants me to study them in their domain, Hitty, not here."

"I know, Brat. I've studied their traditions. A de-briefing of a former CEO will clarify the job requirements. Scrip can reel in your catch."

"Hitty, this mole will begin his graft. I'll slither in to the paving department. That is, if I can coerce a pence or two from you."

"Coercion is not the term to use, Brat, but the scrip is yours. I don't want to miss the outcome."

"I'll wiggle out and begin my campaign. No time like the dark of the moon to do a postmortem."

"The pence are on the tab for you, Brat," she said as he slammed the door on his way out. *I'm growing fond of the youngster and it's not lawful. Hitty, Hitty, get a grip on yourself,* she moaned.

The names of the minor workers flicked through Brat's mind and he decided to approach Beterbe, the one he knew best. He had been snagged in a tangle between Vexy and Swinne and ended up on the road detail.

Brat went to the building where Beterbe lived and waited for him. He came around the corner drooping in weariness and grimy with dust. "What's up old chap?" he said. "Seems eons have passed since I last saw you." He opened his door and motioned Brat into his tiny room.

"Would you mind making us a cup of tea? And bring me a biscuit. The fixings are on the counter next to the hotplate." Beterbe fell onto the bed with a plop. "I'm in dire straits, Brat. That Swinne did me in. I only disagreed with him on how to control Vexy and Hassel."

"Hold on a while longer. Swinne hasn't made a move to fill your position. Likely he's afraid of questions being asked." Brat poured two cups of tea, gave one to Beterbe, then sat down on the bed.

"He will be grilled if he has the nerve to post my position," Beterbe said.

"I have a project that may help us both." Brat said, and described his assignment.

"How much, Brat? One of the fellows I know might be willing to leak a few scraps of info. Have you any pence to give him?"

"I'll scrounge it somehow, Beterbe. Speak to him and let me know."

"His name is Kruknsak. He's been on the job about three years. A pitiful wreck. I have a couple hours off in two more nights. I'll be in touch."

Brat went home by the back alleys and fell into bed. He got up at sunset and studied a few hours.

Umm... a curious lot, the humans, he thought and plowed deeper into the material. *Up my alley,* he said to himself. In the late hours of the night, he took a break. *A visit to Vexy is on order,* he decided.

Vexy opened her door with an ill-tempered look on her face. Hassel lunged by her and disappeared into the night.

"What do you want, Brat." she said in a tone that matched her look.

"I want to thank you, Vexy, for your topnotch leadership."

"Don't overdo it, Brat," she responded in a softer tone.

"I'm not, Vexy," he protested. "Your supervising is the best."

"You go on home now, Brat. I have to deal with the quisling, Hassel, tonight."

Ah-ha, he said to himself, *a point to ponder here. Another Swinne and Vexy plot.*

A stopover at the illustrious twosome might be useful, he thought.

Wim opened the door to his knock and called out, "The studious one is here, Luna."

She tittered and said, "Brat the dutiful, come in and update us on your Earthies."

"Any proposal to amend the minerals yet?" Brat asked as he stepped through the door.

"Don't be flippant; it's not seemly of you, Brat," Luna said in a hurt tone." Seeing as how you interrupted our studies."

"I don't see a book in sight," he said. "Anyway, I came with the aim of pumping for info, not drilling for it."

"Pump and siphon, we're ready," Wim said.

"Any notice of Vexy and Hassel, in particular? They team teach, but do they get on with each other."

"What is this, Brat?" Luna said in a suspicious tone."

"Lighten up, I mean darken up, both of you .Notions of persecution are for our betters not lowly peons like us," he replied.

"We have noticed some spiteful by-plays between them lately," Wim said.

After exchanging a glance with Luna, Wim inquired, "Why are you asking us these questions?"

"Vexy said something that set me to wondering, and I do wonder a lot. Protection is best before the fact than after is my motto."

"You worry too much Brat. Vexy has been our Mentor for ages. She's a bad tempered ninny."

"Forewarned is forearmed my old nanny used to say. Wish I could remember who she was," Brat replied. "However, I'll exit and leave you to your interrupted studies."

Sneaky and deceitful as they are, the twins are no match for Vexy, They're as hopeless as the pathetic humans, Brat thought as he walked home by the side streets.

After a meal of crackers and an apple, he went to bed with the thought, *Starving is not an option. Cadge from Hitty again.* He made a note to call in on Beterbe during the coming night.

Brat arose at dusk and decided to run his dealings of the night before by Hitty. He studied the customs and manners of the humans until past midnight, then he strolled towards her staclet.

"No moon tonight. Certainly pleasant out here, Spadd," he said to a neighbor trudging home from his evening shift on the shovel brigade.

Spadd lifted his weary head and growled, "What's pleasant about it?" And trudged on.

Wonder how Spadd got to be a punch ladle at The Works. He's never in the mood to tell me. He gazed after the retreating figure that walked with a tired stoop amid the flickering red shadows. A forlorn feeling washed over Brat for a moment. He shrugged his shoulders and said to himself. *No place here for such feelings.*

He entered Hitty's door and slammed it behind him.

"Where are you, Hitty?" he yelled as the door opened and hit him in the back.

"Here you are, Brat, for another meal I suppose."

"Not exactly, Hitty, but I wouldn't turn a heavenly one down."

"Heavenly, Brat? You're getting too free with your words. Watch yourself. No permission given to mention the heavens.

"I went across the hall to see Hassel. He's in a blue funk. Vexy and Swinne are excluding him from their meetings, and he suspects trouble is in the offing."

"I suspect trouble isn't a distant traveler and is coming closer to Luna and Wim too. Your warnings to me haven't run off, Hitty. Have you eaten breakfast yet?"

"Hot cereal is on the menu tonight with buttered toast and maybe a little jam. A glass of OJ and a cup of coffee."

"A generous offering, Hitty."

"Don't overdo the generous, Brat. You're on the brink."

"Exactly what Vexy told me last night. While you work on our breakfast, a tale will be offered in payment."

"You are a natural at brashness, Brat. No need of mentoring in that area, or having lessons on how to clean out my bank account."

"Thanks for the tribute, Hitty. I need a bit of feedback on how I'm doing occasionally.

"Now, to my tale. I saw Beterbe at The Works yester night, and he's a pliable reed for my plucking. He'll be in touch tonight, or is it tomorrow night? I can't keep up. The nights go so fast. With all this plotting and scheming I'm getting downright miserable."

"Buck up, young nipper, no room here for misery. Snarl and scowl is the thing. It's adjustment, Brat, that's what it is. Everyone does the dumps. HH makes certain we're all equal in that and everything else. Simplicity in living is his motto, and he trumpets it every night or two from his palatial mansion."

"Well, Beterbe can stoke the furnace with the dumps. They clash with my nature. Bring the food on, Hitty. And by the way, a mite of scrip for the CEO."

"There's no end to your wiles with my scrip and my food, but then I did agree, as if agreement meant much here. How many?"

"Ten pence will do. Mucked up Beterbe and Kruknsak can share it."

"Slink warily, you're in chancy zones, Brat."

"Don't I know it? I slink here, and I sneak there these nights. Where's my food?"

"In front of you. Eat and tell me more about your sneaking."

"I saw Vexy and Hassel on a fact-finding call in. She was in a temper when she opened the door. Hassel was standing behind her in the room. Before she could close the door, he slunk past her, and disappeared into the night. She muttered something about the quisling Hassel and sent me home."

"Clearly, she and Swinne are filing and sanding him down for his appointed fate," Hitty said.

"From Vexy's, I skipped over to see Luna and Wim. Talk about fate. They seem to be hurtling toward theirs like a speeding train."

"It's hard to stop a speeding train, Brat. The wreckage is the stopping point. You've warned them enough."

"The twins are playing with fire, and soon they may be stoking it alongside Spadd." Brat grinned, and emptied his OJ glass. He gazed at Hitty sitting across the table placidly eating her toast. "Mind giving me your extra piece of toast, I have a bit of jam left."

"No limits on your pincers, is there, Brat? A trait to note." She put the toast on his plate and said, "More cereal?"

"No, I'll waddle home and study an hour or two, in case Beterbe drops by. I've scotched my hopping over to see him tonight. I'll take the pence with me, Hitty."

She counted out ten coins from the bowl on the counter. He took them and left without slamming the door behind him.

How the darkness deepens in the young sprig. Hitty thought. Then she returned to the matter of Hassel and Vexy.

Brat hurried home and resumed his studies. He closed his research on CEO'S and tackled investment banking. Mergers and acquisitions caught his attention, and the hours passed until the approach of dawn. *The world of the big cheese; smash and grab. For the Kruknsaks anyhow,* he thought.

With a pot of tea and a box of stale crackers filched from Hitty, he sat ruminating on the fate of Kruknsak until he crawled into bed and fell asleep.

Schemes and Strategies

3

At nightfall, Brat dressed in his one dark costume, put on a black wig, and pasted a mustache on his upper lip.

A worthy way to spend my pence. Whims, not food, he thought. After penciling in a few facial lines he put a folder under his arm, left his staclet, and made his way to Swinne's neighborhood a half mile distant.

He rang the bell, tuned to the shrill scale. A rotund figure appeared in the doorway with a ferocious frown on his face. "I' m in the middle of my beauty routine. What do you want?"

"Sorry to disturb you, Sir. I'm here from the EB on our five-year fact gathering and facility review."

"Oh, please, don't mind me," Swinne simpered. "Come in, come in." He waved Brat towards his settee. "Of course, the Educational Bureau that guides our humble efforts in turning out fit graduates."

"I've noticed your dutiful efforts, Mr. Swinne, since I'm the one receiving your reports at the end of the year. Quite strong overall," Brat said, taking a seat. He opened his file folder and took out his pen. "So strong in fact, I specifically wanted this assignment in order to meet such a model of strength."

"Tea and biscuits, clotted cream and apricot jam for you, Mr....what did you say your name was?"

"My, name? Oh yes, my name. Why it's Slye Cunin if you must know. I'll gladly take your tea, and if you happen to have a sandwich handy I'll take it." Brat motioned to the mini kitchen where the lunch fixings lay on the counter.

"Mr. Swinne, a report reached us recently on two pupils and one of your trainers."

"How can that be when we are forbidden to have any contact with the EB?"

Brat winked at him and said, "How do we know? We have our ways, Mr. Swinne."

Swinne turned ashy through the crust on his face and said, "Excuse me, time to take my facial peel off." He went to a basin by his bed, washed his face, and dried it off. He then went into the kitchen and made the tea and a sandwich of cheese and tomatoes. "Please accept my humble offering Mr. Cunin. Would you like another sandwich?"

"One more will do nicely." Brat replied. "This traveling is extremely tiring."

The sandwich was placed in front of Brat with a large piece of apple cake. "My own recipe, Mr. Cunin, a favorite of mine."

"Mr. Swinne, your talents are spread in many directions.

"Now, about the trainer. Her name is Vexy. I believe she works with a Hassel. Is that correct? And she is Mentor to twins?"

"That's correct, Mr. Cunin. A respectable Mentor so far. She isn't in trouble with the head office, is she? She can be flighty at times, but I'm keeping her on a tight rein."

"Be sure to do so, Mr. Swinne. The report we have can go either way. If she carries out her assignment with these twins as ordered, all will be well. Inform her that we are expecting good reports on the pupils. No trickeries from the Mentor. We need the young buds for our future leaders. And that goes for her team trainer, Hassel."

Swinne's rosy face turned rosier, and he said, "I'll follow instructions to the letter, Mr. Cunin. Don't you worry. She and I will have a scene tonight...I mean conference. I was getting ready to go into the office when you rang my doorbell."

"You are a ready chap, Mr. Swinne. I'll take my exit and leave you to get on with your business. While we're on the topic of business, is your assistant about? What is his name, I forget."

"Beterbe, Mr. Cunin. He's off tonight, but he'll be back tomorrow. These assistants are forever asking for a night off."

"It's so, Mr. Cunin, and we indulge them once a year or so."

Swinne stood up somewhat shaky on his feet and said, "Your visit has been an honor. Let me attend you to the door. May I offer you another sandwich and one of my apple cakes for a later snack, Mr. Cunin?"

"Your offer is accepted, Mr. Swinne. Your delicious treats will not go to waste, I assure you."

<hr />

Brat went off chuckling to himself as he stole home through the back alleys with his freebies. He took his wig and mustache off before entering his room. After washing the marks off his face, he sat deliberating on his next move.

Enough strategy for the present, he thought, and turned to his study of investment banking. *Stocks, bonds, and derivatives, huh? The humans are inventive.*

He studied for a short time, and then he went out to meet with Vexy and the twins.

Luna and Wim weren't in the room and Vexy paced the floor clenching and unclenching her hands.

"Where are the twins?" Brat asked her.

She stopped and said nervously, "They won't be here for tonight's session, Brat. An urgent task arose. It may be a day or so before they return."

"I wonder what could be so momentous for them, Vexy? We know our first duty is to you and Hassel."

"Never you mind, Brat. Hassel is here, so let us get on with our duty to you."

Hassel came through the door with a beaming euphoric smile.

"My dear, Vexy," he said, "Swinne has commended us on our splendid team teaching. He sent his best regards to you. "'You and Vexy are fortunate to have such promising pupils, a star threesome,'" he said to me.

"So there, young Brat," Hassel said, "A citation of approval from our boss. Keep this up and you'll be known in higher circles."

"Hassel, that carrot lures me on. My intentions are to please you and to carry you along with me."

Hassel laughed, "A fanciful young sprout, eh, Vexy?"

Brat reviewed his readings with them for thirty minutes. Then Vexy said, "You're doing very well, Brat. We'll see you tomorrow night. I must run to do a few errands."

She hurriedly put on her jacket and left. Brat glanced at Hassel who had a perplexed look on his face. "I wonder what errands she has to run," he said in a confused tone of voice. "

"Hard to tell with Vexy," Brat replied. "It must be critical for her to scurry out like a fire needing to be quenched."

Hitty requires a visit; I'll drift to her staclet before moving on to Beterbe. Brat said to himself as he took his leave of Hassel and banged on her door soon after.

Hitty sat on the settee with a book in her hands and Brat plopped down beside her. "Don't you have enough influence to get a bigger settee, Hitty? This one is a tight squeeze for the both of us."

"What good is a bigger settee, Brat? For you to bounce on? Anyway, a mender from the hardware is coming to fix my door. A rubber jiggy glued to the door will keep your mitts from destructive bangs."

"A problem solved, Hitty, and I helped you do it. Put it on my tab."

"Your tab is inflating, Brat. You pay or the shovel detail will."

"Let's not talk of inflating tabs, Hitty. I want to know if any news is circulating about the twins. You're a first-rate circulator. No use to deny it."

"I heard they were on the first shift at the ovens this evening. That's about all I can tell you. Vexy whipped out her portfolio on crimes at the EVB last night, and the twins were done in.

"Another thing...Hassel was extra perky before he whisked off to the office tonight. It's not in his nature to be cruel to the pupils, so why was he so perky?" Hitty asked.

"Another curious thing," Brat said, "Vexy was nervous when I got to class. Hassel came in throwing flatteries at us that had been thrown at him by Swinne. It seemed to make Vexy even jumpier. She hurried through our class and left on some errands, or so she said."

"Nights of mystery, Brat. Swinne and Vexy must be in a scrimmage, and between the two, Hassel escaped by the skin of his pointy teeth."

"Whatever it is, I'm glad he escaped. The thought of Vexy being our lone teacher is toxic."

"Toxic may be a thought, but that's all it is. Doesn't do you any good to have it."

"I'll cast it off, Hitty. My studies are bidding me to a diet of crumbs. You don't have a more substantial offering, do you?"

"My middling meal is on the offer, Brat. A veggie soup and my home baked bread. I splurged my pence on them."

"Let's at the eats then. My company is claimed for other places."

"You are a devious imp, Brat, and no circulating needed to find it out," she said as she got up and laid her book aside.

"You won't find me on the circuit, Hitty. I'm under the radar, a lowly form of existence."

"Luna and Wim have been on your mind lately. Best curb any altruistic leanings. Thinking of poking into red hot dealings?"

"Why would I do such a thing, Hitty? As you say, red hot dealings, especially by the vixen."

"Mind yourself. Spies are everywhere and the fledglings are the most zealous."

"I'm on the lookout." Brat said and gave the door an extra hard slam on his exit.

Home first, and then to dusty Beterbe before he's ground into the bricks, he thought.

A short time later, Brat was dressing in grimy overalls and a light brown wig that covered most of his face. Scrip pocketed, he went through the opening he had made underneath the kitchen counter. *Came in handy*, he thought as he came out into the alley and slouched toward Beterbe's staclet. He glimpsed him half way down the block and sidled in his direction. "Pssst," he whispered, "It's me, Brat."

"Meet us at the Horn In pub around the corner in fifteen minutes," Beterbe muttered in passing.

Brat entered the crowded and noisy pub filled with the shift workers basking in their two hours off for the month. He ordered a pint of light beer and found abooth in a dimly lit alcove. He sat drinking his beer and musing on Kruknsak.

He spotted Beterbe coming through the door with a wizened worker who walked with a stoop. He waved them over to his booth, and ordered two large malt whiskies.

"Mr. Kruknsak," Brat began, "I'm indebted to you for granting me an audience. No names will be mentioned or recorded. Your experience in the human world is important for my studies. Of course, you will be paid for your time."

"Yes, I'm willing to sell...uh...supply you with basic facts, young Brat. Best to keep our socializing short. One thing I've noticed in these habitations, hanging out is discouraged unlike my late locale.

"This malt is a prime drink, young Brat. In my former haunts, cases of the malt were stacked to the ceiling. The finest of wines flowed like water. Haut Brion, Lafite, and Mouton Rothschild. were but a few.

"The parties on my ninety-foot yacht lasted for weeks. Compared to the four hundred foot yachts of other CEO's mine was rather minor. But it was decked out with the costliest teak wood and interior luxuries, the best money could buy."

"Business parties, Mr. Kruknsak?"

"Mostly, young Brat."

"Invitations to our yacht parties were sought after by numerous show girls and actors. Pleasing additions to our parties."

"My Mentor has told me that entertainers in the arts are here also. One you might look up is Vexy, if ever a chance arises."

"Not much of a chance here, young Brat. This paving job is a lot longer than the board meetings I attended, and almost as taxing on my constitution."

"The companies you headed Mr. Kruknsak, what exactly were your duties?"

"My duties, young Brat? I excelled in visionary qualities. My communication skills were envied throughout the corporate world. My renowned ability to bring in the cash and hold it responsibly secured us the highest rating in the global markets. I rubbled a few companies and birthed a few, hired, fired and recruited my able son, wife and various other relatives to manage the back offices.

"I left the organization and my CEO position under duress from the Board. They took a dim view of my hiring family members and alleged that I used them to move monies to offshore accounts. They stated I permitted the grandkids to fly the corporate jet to overseas parties. An ordeal that mightily distressed me, young Brat.

"While I was boarding the train for my journey here, my family was boarding the ninety foot yacht to set sail for the islands. That's the gist of my story. I hope it proves useful and brings laudatory comments from your Instructors.

"Is it possible to have another of these malts, young Brat?"

A larger malt in front of him, Kruknsak said, "Best to shelve our session at the present. In these quarters the less information the better in contrast to my late regions. Not as much difference as I imagined though between them. Night instead of day. I worked longer hours in my day job."

"You're an illustration for my studies, Mr. Kruknsak and worth more than the paltry coins I pay you."

"Nay, nay, young Brat, the little here is more than all my able son stashed in the islands. I'll take your coins gladly and introduce you to a friend of mine on the shovel brigade for a pittance more. Beterbe says you're into learning the affairs of investing. If so, the trader Selnby is your source."

Brat handed the coins to him under the table and said, "Your offer is accepted, Mr. Kruknsak. Give me the details of your source next month. I'll be here waiting."

"You may have some good news tonight or the next, Beterbe, in addition to this reward," Brat said while sliding the pence toward him.

A stimulating night, he said to himself, as he wound his way home through the alley and through the back door. He removed his clothes and wig, took a shower and tumbled into bed.

The full-sized moon outside his mini window seemed to smile as its light faded and merged with the rising sun.

Friends and Foes

4

A thump on the door awakened Brat at dusk. He opened his bleary eyes to see Wim in the doorway.

"Wake up, Brat. I have to talk to you. Luna and I have escaped a grisly setup. Last night a security guard came to our room and said our names were on his list. He took us to The Works and someone ordered us to grab a bucket. All night long we carted buckets full of coal to the ovens."

"Slow down, Wim. Let me grab my clothes and make us a cup of tea." Brat washed his face and switched his hot pot on. "A cracker with your tea? My scrip is underwriting other items than food these nights."

"Drink your tea and tell me more," Brat said as he motioned Wim to the table.

"It was awful, Brat, more awful than can be imagined. I thought Luna was going to jump into the fire she was such a basket case. After a while, we were so numb we moved on auto pilot until the six hour shift was over.

We got curious looks from other workers, but no one spoke to us."

"You mentioned setup. What setup?"

"We think it was Vexy, like you warned us. Who else could it be?"

"You may be right. Stick to your studies. Don't give her cause to be vicious to you," Brat said.

"You cautioned us, but we thought you were silly. No more. From here on out, you will be our guide. We won't be idlers in our class assignments either. We learned enough about mineral resources to fill a book last night.

"When the shift ended we staggered outside, and there was Vexy waiting for us."

"'Come with me,'" she said in a muffled voice and led us to our Staclet. Then she ran off without further explanation."

"Time for us to be in class," Brat said. "Are you ready to face the Moira, or the fateful one? How about Luna?"

"Ready or not, here we go, Brat. Stupid as we are, our learning needs a jolt and Vexy is the one to do it."

"Vexy is of the steel variety in educating the un-wary," Brat said. He set the cups on the counter and bagged the cheese-tomato sandwich and apple cake. "A lunch for you courtesy of...never mind," he said.

Luna, still shaky, stood waiting for them in the open door way. She took the items from Brat and looked at him through tear-filled eyes, "I won't let Wim go to class alone. Dreadful hours.... We paid for our foolishness, Brat."

They walked into the classroom and took their seats. Vexy and Hassel were standing near each other and turned at their entrance.

"My dear pupils," Vexy greeted them. She brushed Wim and Luna's cheeks with a kiss. "My lambs we missed you. Welcome back.

"We'll dismiss your present assignment and take up the study of industry if you wish," she said pleasantly.

"Under your guidance, Vexy, the study of mineral resources has been interesting," Wim said. "If you think industry studies will further advance us, then we'll tackle the subject."

"Hassel will direct your lessons for the coming month. I'm slotted into a series of seminars at the Supervisory Institute. Mind Hassel's instructions and do your best while I'm absent."

"Brat, continue your assignment. Your amusing observations enliven my nights. Hassel will send your reports to me."

"And yours too," she said drily to the twins as she took her leave.

For the following hour, Hassel diligently guided them through their lessons. Brat reported on the CEO, Investment Banking sectors, and the differences between them. He didn't mention his interview with Mr.Kruknsak.

The twins added the little they knew of mineral resources, but quite a bit on coal.

Hassel said, "Is coal a special interest of yours? It's usually at the bottom of the list with students. The gemstones are more popular, especially with the feminine class."

"No," Wim said hastily," no interest to us whatsoever. Coal was the first of the mineral resources to attract our attention. Then worry about our relative distracted us."

"We get no marks for worry, Wim. Excuses are not accepted. Don't let it happen again." Hassel said.

"No sir, we won't," Luna said with fervor. "Never, never."

"I saw Beterbe in Mr. Swinne's office as we came in," Brat said. "Did he pass his management exams, Hassel?"

"Evidently, Brat. He's back anyway. He looks a wreck from the struggle. He said the exams were rough. Twelve hours a night. Stop by and say hello to him on your way out."

"Not tonight, Hassel, I have an urgent task," Brat said as he gathered his materials and hurried from the room.

He walked a short distance with the twins who were giddy with delight over Vexy's absence for a month. "We'll be dutiful in our studies," Luna said to him as he separated from them to drop in on Hitty.

"Are you home, Hitty?" Brat yelled as he opened the door and closed it quietly behind him.

"Don't yap so loudly, Brat," Hitty said from the table. "The door business is kaput and now you're drumming for the hearing aid trade."

"Jealousy has grabbed me, Hitty; Hassel stole your attention."

"Hassel seemed peppy tonight and never an explanation as to why," she said. "Was he in class?"

"I'll tell you the tale of Vexy, the vixen, and a scrap of Hassel's woe. It's guesswork, but I noticed that he and Vexy weren't singing the same tune. She and Swinne were palsy, so they plotted grief for Hassel and the twins. In fact, she and Swinne would make a perfect pair of twins. Beterbe, Swinne's assistant went missing too."

"Hold off on Beterbe, Brat, until my agog faculties are fed on Hassel and Vexy."

"The twins, too, Hitty. Anyhow, when we got to class there was Hassel with a big grin on his face. Vexy kissed the twins and gave them another assignment while I sat taking it all in.

"Now for the best news. Vexy will be attending seminars at the Supervisory Institute for the next month, so Hassel will be our lone instructor."

"Worthy news, Brat. I wonder what happened."

"We'll never know, but it's certainly a rally for our flagging morale, Hitty.

"The twins were put to the shovel brigade last night. They wrestled all night with buckets of coal; back and forth, they went to the ovens. Vexy surfaced like the ghoul she is and carted them away at daybreak."

"A gleeful prank of Vexy's, maybe?" Hitty commented. "Curious tricks going on and I don't know. A wonder indeed."

"Whatever was going on, Vexy didn't mean it as a prank," Brat said. "She was too nervous. Wim woke me up beating on my door earlier tonight and told me their story."

Hitty scratched her head and looked at Brat. "Wherever you go there's plenty of drama. How do you do it?"

"No more drama for the twins. They were catapulted from adolescence to a hoary old age in one night. Their frisky stage is over, and in a way, I'll miss their silliness. They were naive, but there's no meanness in them."

"They were fortunate, Brat, to escape Vexy's ire. She's not known in these quarters for generosity." "We're due for some dullness while she's gone. I'll tell you the tale of Beterbe while we feast on your generous provisions. Instantly is my preference."

"My balance is getting pretty low, Brat, and payday is two weeks away."

"Never you mind, Hitty. Serve up your specialty."

"I did make a beef stew and a bread pudding an hour ago. I might have a drop of light beer to accessorize our spread while you talk."

"Before we get to Beterbe, I want an answer to a query that's been bothering me off and on since I arrived here, Hitty. You're an old-timer in these regions and must have noticed these things.

"Human are here in all age groups, but no young ones like the boy I visited. Why is that?"

"Pieces of info I pick up claim the young ones belong to the Supreme Honcho. The humans generate their own young, as the one you saw on your visit. No one can do it here. That's the best answer I have for you, Brat."

"Sufficient for the present, Hitty. The generate thing is in reserve. Do you know much about it?"

"Best to read a book about it, Brat. The Daggie Library has a few books relating to the subject."

"No time, Hitty. A back burner curiosity, so to speak.

"On to Beterbe. He came into the classroom one night and introduced himself as Swinne's assistant. He appeared to be a friendly fellow, but he disappeared a few nights later. By that time, my slinking techniques were on the heavy side. I learned his whereabouts and followed him to his paving job.

"My assignment kicked off, and then you mentioned that CEO's are here. My brain switched to overdrive and I lurked near Beterbe's staclet. I intercepted him as he shuffled home from his work.

"He proved to be a progressive and open to all offers, even the small pence I could give him. We made a deal for an introduction to a CEO on the paving project.

"The raging question now is Kruknsak, the CEO. He remembers being among the Earthlings with a family. How come, Hitty?"

"I can only speculate, Brat. Seems most of the Earthlings who arrive here carry memories of a former existence. I, for one, have only a dim speck of past memories. Even if we wanted to know more we're forbidden to probe into our past."

"My memory is clean gone, Hitty. I recall being on a train with ten others. I saw my form reflected in the light of the train window when we pulled into the station. Panic gripped me in its clutches and didn't let go until you nicked me.

"We got off the train and a Daggie led us down endless stairs to a bunker filled with beds. 'Sleep, until night,' a guard said. We piled onto the single beds and slept as ordered, or like me, tried to still the panic. A bell ringing brought everyone to attention. Then we were led outdoors and chucked into pitch darkness. I was ordered to enter an office nearby. I don't know what happened to the others.

"Someone at a large machine scrolled through sheets of paper. Then she said that staclet number 9 on block 21 was available. I was handed a key along with a sandwich and commanded to take a test. The test was easy, so here I am with you and my other comrades in mischief."

"A glut of memories, Brat. I stood on a corner with a key in one hand and directions in the other to enter staclet number 11 building unit 17. I stood bewildered staring at row upon row of five storied buildings that seemed to have no end.

"The number 17 building was clearly marked right in front of me. I went inside and here I've been ever since. For several years, I directed a section for new arrivals in the educational division. The position of Mentor was posted one night; I jumped and landed it. My IQ rose twenty points when I quit office politics."

"As you said, Hitty, we deal with the given, and this is what we're given. Onwards now to Kruknsak. Delish bread pudding; you've outdone yourself."

"Curb your toady leanings, Brat. Get on with your story."

"Kruknsak and I met in the pub and I quizzed him on his CEO role. The acts that landed him on the pavement job are forbidden in the human world."

Brat shared the details of their meeting and went over his assignment with her. He then mapped his route to the head quarters of the human organization and laid it aside. "I'm perplexed, Hitty. Why do the former humans I'm meeting remember being an Earthie and we can't."

"Put the question on hold and concentrate on your studies, Brat. That's my advice."

"Will do, Hitty. Speaking of studies, I'll stifle the shouting match I'm having with them for another glass of your beer. Kruknsak mentioned wines too. Are there wines here?"

"Wines of all classes are here, Brat. You need scrip to buy them. My pickin's are lean and yours leaner."

"Well then, pickin's must find their way to our door more often, Hitty."

"When their knock comes I'll inform you, Brat. Meanwhile, don't drink all my beer."

"Don't forget to notify me, Hitty. The bit left in the beer bottle is yours. My studies are tugging me home," he said as he attempted to slam the door, which closed quietly behind him.

His thoughts on scrip, he strolled home and dove into his studies.

Four hours later, he ate the last of the crackers and wrote a class report for his CEO assignment.

He took a break and wandered towards the twins staclet to check on Luna.

"Hassel dropped by with an industry reading for us and our heads have been stuck in it for hours. Tea, Brat? Luna said.

"Not to be refused," he replied.

Wim rose from the desk, made tea, and placed the cups on a tray with the leftover apple cake. "Pretty good, Brat, we'll share the last slice. I won't ask where you got it."

"Best not to in our present circumstances. What exactly are you reading in industry?"

"Manufacturing mostly. It's a very boring topic but what can we do?"

"I suggest you talk to Hassel. Perhaps he has some ideas. Seems to me that office staffing might be a better match for you."

"Great, Brat! Luna and I could team in the work. It's a delicate subject. Could you coach us on how to approach Hassel?"

"Begin by inquiries on the course alternatives. Praise his lead teacher skills, and then proceed to ask him if any office programs are open. He's presently high on Swinne's flattery. Best to go now before he recovers."

Brat said bye to the twins and drifted to Beterbe's. "What brings you my way?" he asked on Brat's entrance.

"I passed Swinne's office window and saw you inside, that's what brought me."

"Whatever the reason that landed me back in the office, Brat, I'll never know. Swinne has been irksome in his oily manners, but there's no end to the things I can bear after The Works."

"A light favor then of not much weight. The twins require your magic touch, and I'm certain you will be receptive to their plea."

"I'll listen, Brat. Swinne seems to be on the outs with Vexy so maybe their plea will be granted. While we're on the subject, tell me how you knew I'd get news."

"Silence is an item to be revered in this country, Beterbe. Let us revere it," Brat replied.

On his way home, Brat stopped at his neighborhood grocery to buy a box of crackers. "Hitty's lone farthing," he said as he emptied his pocket and passed the coin to the clerk.

The rising sun on the horizon reminded him to check the time. At home, he brewed a cup of his special tea and reviewed the night's events. *So far, so good, a prome-nade among the wildings next,* he thought as he floated off to sleep.

Among the Wildings

5

Brat awoke at nightfall, washed, dressed for his journey, and raided his savings jar. He wrapped himself in his tunic and crossed over to the Husslm HQ's. *The humans work at night too,* he thought as he entered the building flooded with light. *Info on elevators proved useful.* He moved to the elevators, pushed a button, and ascended to the tenth floor.

Soft lights in the corridor led into a large room with an oversized cherry wood table. An immense chandelier hung from the ceiling and cast dancing reflections on the gleaming wood. A pair of French Ormolu candelabras were lit and positioned along its length. Twelve chairs with seats in red velvet encircled the table.

On the walls were three paintings that drew Brat's attention. *Colorful,* he thought. *Those paintings might enrich Hitty's room.*

He noted the names of the artists. Two were signed Picasso and the other Matisse.

A team of white coated humans placed a pristine linen cloth on the table. Then, thin china plates and silverware were placed along the table with three crystal glasses at each plate. Others were busy setting out hors d'oeuvres on a side table. Wines, white and red, were in buckets of ice on top of a corner cabinet.

He read the name tags, and when he came to Husslm's name at the head of the table, he sat down to check the entrance.

He heard a ting-a-ling, and a door opened in the foyer. A portly man dressed in a dark blue suit and tie strode through the door.

Husslm, the kingpin of the outfit, Brat thought as he watched the man inspect the table arrangements. Husslm turned with a scowl and barked at the women dressed in white, "Finish, and get out."

They hurriedly tripped here and there and withdrew from the room.

Husslm walked towards Brat who hastily moved from the chair. The man poured himself a glass of red wine, tasted it, licked his lips, and growled..."Earthy wine."

Brat moved to check on the ice buckets and read the names of the wines. Chateau Lafite and Screaming Eagle. He stuck his hands in the ice and jerked them out, *Like fire. Wish I could take a piece to Hitty,* he thought. He reached for a tidbit of smoked salmon, then he dipped into the caviar.

Suddenly, four ting-a-lings went off in the foyer, and eight men ranging in size from short to tall came into the room. Their dress varied only from Husslm's by the tie color or the pin striping on their suits. Husslm sprang to his feet and joined their chattering with slaps on the back.

Brat inspected the two candelabras on the table, which had been lit and were now glowing with an orange flame. He went closer and blew out the one nearest to him. *Too much glare in here,* he thought, and blew out the second one. He saw Husslm's half-filled glass of wine and drank it. *A heady stimulator,* he said to himself as the wine hit him in a spinning punch.

A slender woman dressed in a burgundy outfit with a slinky look entered the room. Her dark hair was gathered in a topknot, which gave her face a severe expression. The men immediately came to attention and vied with each other to take her coat. She ignored them after a brief greeting and took a seat. She demurely tucked her skirt over her knees while looking at the men with silver colored eyes.

Husslm stepped to the head of the table and peered at a miniature ornate clock framed in gold. "A quorum is present, so let's wind our business up," he said. "An important appointment is in the offing." He pushed a buzzer, and a woman dressed in white came in, poured more wine into the glasses, and scurried from the room.

After dinner when the wait staff had cleared the table, Husslm called the meeting to order. He said, "We'll have our short meeting here instead of the conference room. " Ms. Buetee, will you read the minutes?"

The minutes accepted, and prior business matters over, Husslm spoke, "Now to new business. Shareholder interests were on the agenda, but as time is limited, we'll discuss the pressing issue of company compensation. Shareholder interests will be revisited at our next quarterly meeting."

Ms. Buetee said. "I take exception to our tabling shareholder interests. Let my dissent be recorded."

"Aye, aye," someone else said.

"Noted," Mr. Husslm said. "The Board's comp is included in the hash...ahem... discussion."

"In that case," Ms. Buetee said, "Weezl and I rescind our objection."

Everyone nodded his or her heads. "Approval noted and seconded by Weezl," Husslm said.

"Financial report, Mr. Luter?" Husslm glanced to the number three seat and saw the unlit candelabras. He bounded up from his chair and went out. His voice penetrated the room in a high-pitched frenzy. He came back in with a red face muttering, "Dumb help."

Mr. Luter gave his report of the profits from the various companies with the failure of one company necessitating the layoff of the workers. "Our companies have underperformed this year, but the failed company has been sold, thereby replenishing our coffers. The workers have agreed to reduce their pay by one dollar per hour. Profits will increase as a result."

"Any comments on the failure or the layoffs?" Husslm asked.

No one spoke.

Mr. Conn raised his hand," I move to accept the financial report."

"Seconded," Mr. Cheter said.

Heads wagged in approval.

Husslm said, "Thank you, Luter, for your encouraging report. I am proposing to award compensation, not only to me, but also to all our directors who secured our objectives. An additional twenty-five thousand dollars is recommended for each of our Board members yearly."

"Votes for approval?"

"Aye, Aye," everyone said.

"Seconded," Ms. Buetee said.

"Business is settled then," Mr. Husslm said. "Move to conclude the meeting?"

"I do so move," Mr. Bogis said.

Meanwhile, Brat had been up and down the table sipping from the wine glasses. He grew dizzy and the forms around the table grew blurry. He leaned over to take a sip from Ms. Buetee's glass and fell onto her lap. She recoiled, stood up, and Brat toppled to the floor while the others stared at her.

"Please excuse me; I'm due home within the hour." She grabbed her coat and rushed from the room.

"Wonder what that was about?" Mr. Letcher said. "She's a tasty...uh... a tasteful woman, very classy.

He made a smacking sound with his mouth and said, "Husslm, are we on for our appointment? No time to waste. Let's wing it."

Brat sat upright on the floor woozily thinking. *She and Vexy are rushers. A feminine trait, I suppose.*

He heard the word "wing" and got himself upright again. *Didn't know they could fly like us,* he thought.

"Cheter, Conn and Bogis are with us, Letcher. The limousine is waiting." Husslm moved into the foyer, everybody followed and Brat did too. They emerged into the street where a light rain was falling. Brat piled into the limo along with the other five. "To the Airport, Lakey," Husslm barked.

Water falls from the sky here, Brat thought as he inspected the interior of the limousine. *Bigger than my staclet. No wheels on mine though.*

"Saw Ole Sloane the other day," Husslm said. "He remarked on a Journal article he had read the day before on Husslm industries.

"I dismissed the article with the comment that the business of the Journal is to criticize successful companies. It's a compliment. Ole Sloane, a sour expression on his face, crossed to the opposite side of the street. He's a prune, one of the old school. Can't keep up with the business methods of this younger generation."

"Hear, hear," the men bellowed. "Party tonight to celebrate our shrewdness."

"Brought any of the wine, Husslm?" Letcher asked.

"Stocked full in the fridge and a Scotch whiskey too. Can you reach it?"

Bogis handed a glass to each and opened a bottle of wine. Brat abstained. *Enough for me,* he thought. *The effects don't suit a Daggie.*

By the end of the first drink, the limo stopped at a field where a plane sat on the runway emitting loud noises. The driver took some bags from the trunk of the Limo, handed them to the men, and drove off. The group marched to the plane and up the stairs. Brat went through the door, found a seat, and inspected the interior.

"Seats eight," Mr. Husslm said, "my Bizjet. Get comfortable. We'll soon see the lights of Vegas." He stepped to the front of the plane and said, "Ready for take-off, Piers."

Conn almost sat on Brat who gave him a hard blow on his rear end. *Not on me. I'm not moving,* Brat muttered to himself.

Conn danced a little jig from the pain while the others roared with laughter. He rubbed himself vigorously and said, "A moment's trouble with a war wound."

"War wound?" Bogis replied. "More likely your wife gave it to you."

"Ha-ha-ha," everyone howled.

"Have another drink, Conn." Husslm said, and added wine to his glass. He then dimmed the lights and the seats were folded into beds. The five men were shortly snoring and snuffling in their sleep.

Brat, tired from the unusual activity of his evening, nicked a blanket off Conn and joined the five in a snuffling slumber.

Brat awoke as the plane descended. Below him were lights glittering amid a bare sandy landscape. *Looks like The Works,* he thought as the plane landed.

The men entered another limo and in a short time, Brat found himself at a desk in an immense building. "Reservations, the Penthouse and four suites for a party of five," Husslm said haughtily.

The crew of bellhops escorted them to their rooms with the luggage. *Only five skinny bags and too heavy for the Earthies to carry,* Brat thought as they got off the elevator on the tenth floor.

Brat continued with Husslm to the twelfth floor. The bellhop led them into a two-bedroom suite that over-looked the lights below. Husslm directed the bellhop to take his pants and shirt downstairs to be pressed. He gave him coins and dismissed him.

A private bedroom for me. Big enough for eight sta-clets. Wish Hitty was here, Brat thought. He lay on the bed and thought of home and his cozy staclet. The sound of water running in the other room intruded into his musings, and he went to investigate. Husslm was in a glass case, soaping himself and humming a tune.

A knock on the door interrupted his crooning. He stepped from the shower, wrapped a towel about himself, and went to the door. Freshly pressed garments were passed to him in exchange for coins, and he carried them to his bed.

A shower for me too, Brat thought, and promptly went to the one in his bedroom. He undressed, wrangled a small table underneath the shower, and turned the water on. He adjusted the water to his liking and took his shower. *A deluxe bath. Wish we had one.*

He grabbed a towel, dried off, and dressed. *I forgot to bring extra clothes. Not that I need any.* Distracted, he idly tossed his hoodie back, and Husslm's eyes and head shaking went haywire.

What the man saw as he gazed into the bedroom was a pale floating face, heart shaped with a sharp chin, two triangular ears between dark spiky hair, and slanted eyes of a crimson hue.

Brat hastily drew the hoodie over his face, and Husslm shook his head as if to clear it and mumbled, "Drinking too much. Better go eat." He hurriedly dressed in his newly ironed pants and a cashmere sweater while grousing to himself, "I gotta get a grip."

He checked his wallet, locked his door, and went into the hallway with Brat right behind him. He pushed a button and they entered an elevator that stopped at the fifth floor. A stocky man of mid-age got on. "Kruknsak Jr.!" Husslm exclaimed. "Read about your father's death. Sorry to hear it, a great business man."

The man stammered, "Thank you."

Brat's interest edged up a notch as he observed the man, a younger version of the elder Kruknsak.

When the elevator halted on the first floor, the man promptly took his leave and vanished in the direction of the Casino.

Husslm's cohorts were at the dining room bar. The headwaiter approached and summoned a hostess to seat them. She escorted them to a table reserved in advance. She was in a short skirt and blouse with sixty percent cleavage. *Not enough coins to buy the clothes she needs,* Brat thought while counting the chairs. *The top of the table for me.*

The five men ordered red wine and put in their orders for prime filet mignons with the trimmings. *These men run on wine, and it takes a barrel for a fill up,* Brat thought as he ensconced himself among the flowers and candles.

Their orders taken, the hostess moved among them filling the wine glasses. Letcher reached out a hand to touch her cleavage, and she backed off. Brat saw the interchange. *None of that here. If you want a touch a slap will do.* He leaned forward and hit Letcher on the side of his neck.

Letcher, bright red in the face, said, "Silly woman hit me."

The others laughed uproariously. "Ticks you off, does she Letcher? Next time keep your paws to yourself," Husslm said. "We're here to have a go at the gaming, nothing else."

The arrival of their orders put a stop to the razzing, and the men concentrated on eating. Brat glanced at their food and decided he'd have bits of the steaks. He made the rounds and filled a napkin of remnants to eat later in the bedroom.

Hunger sated, the men resumed their yakking. "Ready, boys. I'll have a go at roulette," Husslm said.

"Baccarat for me and craps for Letcher," Bogis said.

"Don't forget we leave at 4 pm. My son's birthday party. The wife will have my head if I don't show," Cheter said.

Each of them wandered off, and Brat tailed Husslm to the casino. The deafening noise of the jingling in the dim setting reminded him of Kruknsak Sr.. *Kruknsak was right,* he thought. *The human world and the Daggie world have a mix of qualities in common.*

Husslm moved to a window and exchanged green paper and coins for chips. He then went directly to the roulette table.

Brat scrutinized the interior of the room with the thought, *I think I'll tour the circuit for Kruknsak Jr..* He was sitting among a group of men playing cards. Brat closed in on him and whispered, "Pssst...able son, I know your father. Go to the cafe outside the casino. I'll meet you there."

Kruknsak Jr. lowered his head, finished the game with trembling hands, and rushed from the room.

Brat, already in the cafe, saw him pause and look inside. He hesitantly came in and took a seat. Brat spoke in a low voice, "Don't be scared, able son. Listen to me. Your father is assisting me, so I will assist you. And maybe you can aid me in a vital task."

Brat laid three thin triangular coins imprinted with a 5, 10, and 20 on the table. "I need two pounds of these copper coins and they have to be exact copies." Kruknsak Jr. stared at the coins, and with teeth chattering, gibbered, "I'll never ever come here again. I'll sell the yacht and go into business."

"Be certain to consult Ole Sloane when you do. And hire the hostess from the dining room. She needs clothes for her casing.

"Do you know how to get the coins, able son?"

"I think so. A friend has a games business on the outskirts of Las Vegas. He mass-produces supplies, including coins, for hobby groups." He pulled a gadget from his coat pocket, pushed a button, and began to talk to someone.

"We planned to meet for dinner, but earlier it is," Kruknsak Jr. said. He put the phone back into his coat pocket with the comment, "And here I am talking to myself."

And he's terrified because he can't see me, Brat thought. *I can't see anyone he's talking to on the gadget.*

"No need to fear me, Kruknsak Jr. I want the coins before 4 pm today. Do you have enough money for them? Your father could use a bit for his monthly malt treat."

"No problem. I'll meet you here at 3 pm." He took the coins and scurried out the door.

The light filtering through the window indicated early morning and reminded Brat of sleeping. *First to Husslm and his pals.*

No breaks or stops were evident in their devotion to the games of chance. Each of them wore a long face. Brat went to the lobby, took the elevator to his room, removed his tunic, and dove into bed. *Husslm had better not look in while I'm snoozing,* he thought drowsily.

Brought awake by a loud snore, Brat glanced at the bedside clock. 2:15 pm. He got out of bed, ate his food, washed his face, and donned his tunic. Husslm lay on top of his bed puffing and whistling with deep breathings. *The man has rattled his casing by chancy takings,* he said to himself.

Downstairs, he lingered outside the cafe, waiting for Kruknsak Jr. *Able son had better not do a runner on me,* Brat thought as he searched the area. All was quiet except for lone passersby at intervals. At 3:30 pm, a man sped towards him down a corridor of shops with quickening steps.

"Pssst...I'm outside the doorway," Brat said, taking hold of the man's sleeve.

"Then, take the blasted things," the man said. "An awful day, I've had of it."

Brat opened the satchel and inspected the coins. The copies were faultless. He said, "As ordered, Kruknsak Jr. I'll update your father on your activities. The coins will cheer his nights on the road project." He stowed the packets under his tunic while the man's eyes grew rounder and wider.

"Kruknsak Jr., I advise you to visit Ole Sloane at once and get your future going. Your father will be pleased, and I'll keep him posted on your progress."

A gray cast flooded the man's face. His words, slurred in a gasp, came from frozen lips, "Ole Sloane is on the agenda for this evening." He put one foot behind him, pivoted, and began running.

Brat's watch indicated the approach of 4 pm. He went to the lobby and saw Husslm exit the front door and get in a limousine. *Hah, you're not leaving me here, I didn't map my route home from Las Vegas.* He zoomed into the vehicle and sat in a rear seat to eat the fragments of food garnered from the buffet.

The other men piled into the forward seats without mishap from Brat. Quietness reigned throughout the return trip. Occasionally intermittent snores disturbed the stillness.

Their green paper money ended in glumness. Brat thought. *My coins are enough for me. No Vegas where I live.*

On landing, Husslm said, "Don't forget our conference in Monte Carlo, boys."

"Wouldn't miss it," Letcher said. "No way," Bogis boomed. They all scattered and Brat did too. *I feel pity for them, even if pity is forbidden,* he thought.

Home Doings

6

Brat arrived home two hours later having made a stop at the neighborhood grocery store. Special teas for Hitty and coffee for espresso.

He put the items in the kitchen cabinet, and then wrote his case notes for Hassel and Vexy. He finished and rose from his desk chair to examine the room. He sawed, punched and sanded for some time behind his bed. Satisfied with the result, he crammed the coins inside the space.

Now for the twins and to class, he said to himself. He reached Block 31 and rapped on the door of Staclet 12. A subdued Luna said, "Where have you been, Brat? We don't do well without you."

"Brat, come in, and hear the latest." Wim said. "Our news is a stunner."

Their books and classroom materials were on the desk implying serious study time.

"Busy, eh?" Brat said to Luna.

"No longer goof balls. We want to be studious like you, Brat."

They sat in cordial ease, drinking tea while Wim spoke of their course change.

"Hassel arranged it with Swinne's permission. To lessen Vexy's pique, he gained her consent. She's pleased and states that it was her idea all along."

"We like the office studies and the hours of reading go by fast." Luna said.

Wim cut in, "The classroom beckons, you guys. A pleasant break in the study routine. The dread feeling holding us tightly in its grasp fled the scene with Vexy."

Luna put the tea things away, picked up her assignment, and locked the door behind them.

"A neighbor has the habit of dropping in periodically," she explained to Brat. He looked at her with inquiring eyes. "We're practicing to think ahead like you do."

"Watch the dropping in. It's frowned on, Brat commented.

"We're listening, Brat." Luna said.

With notes in hand, they entered the classroom to be greeted by Beterbe. "Hassel has invited me to a sit-in tonight. Hope you don't mind."

"No objections, Beterbe," Brat said.

"None from us," Luna said.

Hassel appeared with class supplies in hand, and began the session.

The twins gave lengthy reports and he recorded their progress on a flow chart.

"You've got the hang of it," Hassel said. "Continue your readings for a couple of weeks before a quiz."

Brat read condensed notes of his journey to the Earthlings and said, "A peculiar bunch. The group I observed weren't pleased with their junket."

"I'm not learned in the area, Brat. Check the history of human foibles for an answer. Arrange your visitation and studies as you please. Maybe an answer will surface."

Hassel dismissed them with a remark from Beterbe, "Presentations well-done."

Brat and the twins walked home leisurely and parted at his staclet. "Come by tomorrow night. Don't forget," Luna said.

⸻

Self-reliance is a trait unknown to the twins, Brat thought as he walked home. He placed the coffee and a bag of coins inside his shirt and made his way to Hitty's.

"There you are, Hitty," he said as he came through the door.

Hitty sat on the settee, a bulky tome on humans in her lap, paused and looked at him. She put the book aside and got up. "You still fancy my company after being with the Earthies the entire night."

"The world of the humans is a riotous ruin, and I don't think the environs produced me. I visited only a few, but I reckon they could be partners of our Head Honcho any night."

"Deep thinking is to be avoided, Brat. What's the lighter side of your trip?"

"I brought something back for you, Hitty. Gander at this." He removed the coins from his shirt and placed them on the table.

She jiggled the package while she gazed at him. She reached inside, felt the coins, and pulled one from the bag.

"Brat, are you meddling in a mischief that will guarantee us a five year sentence on the road detail?"

"No, Hitty, they came from a human. Kruknsak Sr.'s son tended to the coining chore. A pound for you and a pound for me. No forgery to admit to. Aren't we expected to have ingenuity?"

"Cunning and conniving, Brat? No questions asked or answers given. You do pay your debts in lavish amounts."

"By chance, Hitty. Penury needs a rest from its spat with us. Give the coins repose in a safe area. A few will buy us an espresso machine."

"Never you mind, Brat. I have a safe spot, and you will have an espresso pot. A shopping spree in another Ward is due. Your input is the coffee.

"Brat, you and I are standing on a minefield greater than a Vexy ordeal. We are transgressors and liable for a term in the re-education department."

"What is re-education?"

"Daggie term of being sent to toil in some drudge work. Where is beyond me. We'll not refer to this conversation in the future. Hear me?"

"I hear, I hear, Hitty."

She listened to his travel account while they ate. Brat said, "I want to tell you something, Hitty. The human feeling termed pity came over me while I was with Husslm. I've tried to shrug it off, but it's still with me."

"There's no term for pity here, Brat. I can't give you advice on it. I suspect it's unknown and forbidden. Best watch yourself."

"Watchful it is. My next observation is a politician. I'll postpone the investment banker task. The agenda for the next two weeks is study. If my other assignments go smoothly, it may be a short year."

"Don't decree a split with troubles any time soon, Brat. Going smoothly is unknown in this district."

"I'll keep a lookout, Hitty, and avoid the Daggie attractions to trouble."

"We Daggies' have far less attractions than the humans. Aspiring to the upper echelon is the main one here. Troubles come in mammoth lots, if candidates are detected."

"I'm not a fan of the upper echelons, Hitty."

"I'm instructing you on how to avoid trouble, Brat, by keeping pity to yourself."

"No tone deafness in my ears, Hitty. I'll leave you now to your mentoring precepts until the dusk falls on the daylight again."

The humans are sent here for being lawless, and here I am feeling pity for them, Brat thought on entering his staclet.

He checked on his coins in the cranny, took a bath, and dropped into bed.

He awoke at nightfall, ate breakfast, and made a pot of coffee. He then studied for an hour and set his book aside. *I'll pop in to see the twins before the politicians get me,* he thought.

He stepped into the busy street filled with his neighbors leaving for work. No one spoke or greeted him as they diverged and plodded away in various directions. *Kruknsak Sr. said it. The Daggies aren't a sociable folk. 'Forbid' is the creed of HH.*

Luna and Wim sat at their desk absorbed in study. Their faces glowed as they turned to him. "Brat, this course is so interesting we can scarcely believe our fortune."

Luna said. "Please, do the teas and my special bread for you."

"She timed out to bake the bread, Brat," Wim said. "We have one more paragraph before we break." "The twins in serious mode," Brat commented while making the tea and setting the tray on the table with nicely browned bread.

He sat and listened to their ravings and nodded his approval at intervals. "Your niche exactly. Office personnel work. And speaking of niches, do you have any memory clips before arriving here?"

Both stared at him for a moment, and then Wim said, "Why ask us the question, Brat?"

"Hitty and I were on the topic, and I wondered if your experience was similar to ours?"

"We never mention the subject, Brat. We have a brief memory of an accident before awakening here. We don't know further than that."

"That's four of us. Too much to be a coincidence. A mystery for the solving."

"For you maybe. We're so busy we don't have time to wonder."

"A future task, my lovelies. I'm off to my studies now. When shall we three meet again at Hassel's behest?"

"Don't tease Brat. The morrow night it is," Luna replied.

As he approached his staclet, Spadd passed him on his way to The Works, "Good evening, young Brat," he said cheerily with a slight smile on his coal smudged face.

"A fine night, Spadd," Brat returned. "You look chipper in this vitalizing air."

"I've been promoted, young fellow, and it's vitalizing enough for me. I'm Stoker number one. It's a little warm, but a notch above the shovel brigade with a six hour shift instead of eight."

"Enough said, Spadd."

He stood and watched Spadd's sprightly steps as he vanished around the corner, all four feet of him appeared taller and stronger.

In honor of politicians and Spadd's promotion, I'll toast them with a white tea; he lifted his cup, took a sip, and embarked on his studies.

The darkness faded into glimmers of light before he tore himself away and went to bed. *Politicians exercise a variety of stratagems to attain their ends. More than the CEO's do,* he thought as he fell asleep.

He awoke at sundown, showered, dressed, and went to the twins. They walked to class through empty streets mutely watching the flickering red shadows dancing on the buildings.

On their entrance to the classroom, Brat saw Beterbe in Swinne's office, which reminded him of Kruknsak. Must ask for some info from Beterbe.

He and the twin's gave reports, went over their assignments with Hassel, and separated shortly after their class dismissal.

"Hassel is assigning us to an office setting before Vexy get's back. Isn't that great, Brat?" Luna said.

"Indeed, it is. Hitty could give you some pointers on offices to select, if you wish?"

"Oh, would she, Brat? We haven't the faintest idea about offices."

"A check on her availability is my priority. I'll let you know."

He loitered near Beterbe's building until he walked into view and followed him inside.

At his knock, Beterbe opened his door with a hearty, "Brat, what are you doing here?"

"To obtain info from you. Kruknsak is from the world of the humans?"

"He is, Brat. Is it wise to ask these things? We are forbidden to talk about the origins of the residents."

"Between us, Beterbe. Are you an expat from the human world?"

"I do have hazy memories of a home and family, but I'm not certain. It's been so long ago. Our country is filled with numerous humans. That I know. The Works and the Pavement project employ lots of them. And there is the railway."

"Your info is secure, Beterbe."

"Anytime, Brat. Kruknsak is looking forward to your meeting in a couple of weeks."

"Guess you can't go to the pub with me?"

"I daren't, Brat. Too risky."

"Okay, I'll be off. Tell me, have you eaten Swinne's luscious apple cake?"

"No, why do you ask?"

"Rumors from an unknown source."

For the next two weeks, Brat concentrated on his studies with intermittent visits to Hitty and classroom attendance. In the meanwhile, the twins had a session with Hitty and took her advice to enter a program for staff management. Hassel had experience in the program and became their Mentor with Vexy's approval.

Time to do some fieldwork, Brat said to himself on the evening he finished his studies. He dressed in the work clothes, wig of his previous pub visit, and put a handful of coins in his pocket. *Kruknsak Sr. is getting a treat,* he thought.

On entering the pub, Brat spotted him and edged through the crowd to sit down across from him. "Mighty doings since I saw you last."

"Wish I could say the same, young Brat. Polishing off a pile of bricks is big doings for me."

"A stellar performance on your job?"

"Even so. I'm allowed three hours at the pub for the deed."

"Add a fill- in on your able son."

"Young Brat, don't joke with me. I'm not up to a sham in these parts."

"No tricks, Kruknsak Sr.. I met your son in the human world. He's decided to sell out and start a business. He's consulting Ole Sloane who will steer him in the venture."

"The best news I've heard since setting my feet on this plane." He glanced down at his shoes, "An improvement overall."

"Absolutely," Brat said. "Your able son sent you some coins for your malt."

"Treats are things unknown in this region, but slip them to me any old time."

"Will do." Brat lowered his voice and said, "I've postponed meeting the investment banker in favor of a politician. Don't happen to know any of those, do you?"

"Can't say I do, young Brat. Most politicians work on the railroad and the lower levels. You might consult Seeznsken who was a trader in high finance. He was a regular on the Pipeline detail."

"The unit is a lower level one?"

"Aye, it is. The sewer level. He was assigned to the pavement job a month ago. A step up for him."

"A step up in more ways than one, eh?"

"Positively, young Brat."

"Would you mind giving me his staclet number and the one for Selnby? Yours too. Might come in handy some night."

"Building 226, unit 21. Seeznsken likes company though it's forbidden in this country. Selnby lives in Building 213, unit 23. Mine is Building 206, unit 15."

"I'm in your debt, Kruknsak Sr., I'll see you in a month."

Brat memorized the numbers, gave him the coins, and then strolled to Hitty's. She was at her tiny stove stirring a pot of beans and chili.

"Cornbread with the chili, Hitty?"

"Already for you, Brat. Needs warming. Light beer is on the counter top. Can't be seen spending too freely."

"Take while the takings are offered, Hitty. And I am."

"You've earned my liberal bounty, Brat. Not another word or I'll boot you through the door."

"No words from me. See my lips are zipped."

He then described his latest tryst with Kruknsak Sr. and his plans to meet Seeznsken. "Information on a politician's work is what I'm after."

"When you gain the info, enlighten me. My curiosity is craving a treat."

"You know where curiosity got the Cheshire cat, Hitty."

"Actually, I don't, Brat. What did the Cheshire cat get?"

"Don't ask me, Hitty. It disappeared is all I know."

"I'll try not to disappear anytime in the near future. Scoot now, and let me go through my beauty routine before bed-time."

Brat went home, studied politics for an hour, and then went to bed. *Hitty's beauty routine? What's that?* He thought as he sank into sleep.

Curiosity

7

Hitty sat engrossed in thought after Brat went out the door forgoing his usual attempt to slam it. *The young spratling needs watching, and I'm not a watcher. He's up to something. Time for a visit with Sadie, my ex-pal from the office.* She took a shower and hurried through her weekly beauty routine. She did a face mask, washed it off, and then creamed her face and body.

She put her robe on and made plans for the next night. *First, the grapevine—had better see Bittsy.* Tactics in place, she changed clothes and went to the third floor with a packet of tea in her hand. The occupant of the end unit 301 opened to her knock. The figure in the doorway stood three feet tall with a halo of flaming red hair. In a fluttery voice she said, "A passing visit, Hitty?

"Barging in isn't my style, but I'm in need of your help, Bittsy. Brew a pot of this tea and let's get talking. You're the master at fact gathering and everything in between." While Bittsy made the tea and placed the cups on the table, Hitty sat and looked at her. She waited until the tea was poured and Bittsy was sitting at the table.

"Any current rumors flying in the underground?"

"None fresh that I know of, Hitty. The only one of interest is the upcoming visit from our Head Honcho."

"Oh, is he? And when is that to be?"

"Not certain. As usual he never tells us, but we're guessing his staff will arrive in three months or less."

"You can expect a lot of groans and laments also."

"Higher ups than me can do them, Hitty. Bottom of the totem polers get a brief glimpse of him while he rolls through town in a pink or red Bugatti convertible.

"He does like to give the security forces a hint of what awaits us if we don't keep our paws and maws under control. The flames carved on the side of his Bugatti aren't wasted on us."

"The same old thing, huh? He wheeled into town in a fluorescent red Bugatti about the time I arrived. What a dunder head I was, gawking and staring. Not a glimpse of his black booted feet since."

"One roll-in is enough to remind us who's boss. Glad we live in a corner where he seldom visits."

"Agreed, Bittsy. He's not the chatting type with that dark scowling face of his and his black tunic whooshing in the car's whirlwind."

"The whirlwind in our office is enough for me. My promotion to Internal Affairs is a mixed bag. The extra foot of space in my unit is useless. I liked it better when we worked in the Residential and Labor Department."

"Yes, but shifting personnel was in the air when I latched on to the Mentoring assignment."

"I'd like a shifting out in this assignment. The politics in Internal Affairs is squally and variable. It's a venue for hoof and mouth disease. You have a great job, Hitty. How did you nab it?"

"At the opportune moment. Keep your eyes open and your head low. That red hair of yours is hard to miss."

"One of my best features. I cover my hair when I'm working. Best toddle away now. We don't want to be caught in a tete-a-tete."

"One more thing and I'll scurry home. Do you know anyone who takes side jobs in security affairs?"

"Sadie is in the Internal Security section now. She might be the one to ask. Confidentially, one skulks in after hours. He lives in Building 71, unit 67, name of Prye. You might catch him on his break. He's home for two nights."

"Off I go then, Bitsy. Share is on the table when your favor is due. By the way, what is the difference between the Security sections?"

"We focus on administration while Internal Security's function is to keep public order."

"No lack in the order of the public, Bitsy, but why not call it External Security?"

"Don't ask me, Hitty. The higher-ups say Internal Security is applied to the whole country."

"Back to my inner sanctum, then."

Hitty scuttled home and into bed with the thought, *Hah! Your secrets are to be outed,* Brat. She fell asleep and dreamed of losing her bag of coins in Las Vegas.

Brat was up early the next night engrossed in the captivating life of a politician. His readings on the forms of government in the human world magnified his interest. *Democracy? All I remember is this one, and it's an autocracy run by the colossus. No elections here,* he said to himself.

His watch indicated class time. He laid aside his book, grabbed an apple, and set off for the twins staclet.

While chewing on his apple, the thought occurred to him, *Apples grow on trees. There are no apple trees in Daganland. Hitty has some explaining to do.*

The twins were ready to go when he knocked on their door. They ambled through the streets filled with departing workers bound for their shift at The Works.

No one spoke to them, but many noticed the bubbly Luna nattering about how much she liked the office program. Brat shushed her with a finger to his lips.

Hassel was cheerful throughout their lesson reviews, but at dismissal, his mood became gloomy. "Vexy is due home within a week, and we'll have to...I mean, we will welcome her back," he said.

Brat and the twins walked home with dampened spirits. "We'll cope, never fear," he said.

"With what, Brat? We don't have any copers," Luna said.

"Maybe she did so well in her seminar exams she got promoted. She's a very smart Daggie, and the angles are not unknown to her."

"A hope is all we can muster," Wim said. They parted at the twins unit while Brat walked home thinking of Vexy and her schemes.

Must be some way to deal with her. Can't use the throttling method. Wits must serve to curb her whims.

He went home and changed into his grubby pair of overalls. He then put his mustache on and attached a wig of gray hair to his head on. And shortly a hunched over figure stole silently through the back alleys to Building 226. He knocked on the door of unit 21, and in return, a quavering whisper came, "Who is it?"

"It's me," Brat hissed. "Kruknsak sent me." The door opened and he slipped in.

"I don't have but a minute, young Brat, I daren't be late at the paving works," Seeznsken said. "How can I help you?"

"Any info on human politicians?"

"I was involved in a few campaigns, and one added to my sentence here. Though it's best, you see Polwin on the lower pipeline project in Building, 313, unit 39. His politics led him into important offices. Must have been lofty, his sentence in the lower regions runs ten more years. I stayed three years and got a transfer to the upper regions a month ago."

"Your info will be used discreetly, Seeznsken. Will a meeting be possible to discuss investment banking? Bank- ing is your forte, Kruknsak said."

"If Kruknsak referred you to me, I'll provide you with the sordid details of my transgressions, young Brat. Check back with me in a month. I'll have one job not two."

"Will do. I'll look up Polwin in the meantime. Does he live in the lower regions?"

"Near the entrance, young Brat, as you emerge from the central elevator. His Building is the first on your right."

"You are helpful, Mr. Seeznsken. May I offer you a pence for a malt?"

"Gladly. Pence are at a premium in these parts. I get an hour off next week. I'll drink to your health with Kruknsak. He's to join me in celebrating his brick making skills."

Brat gave him two coins and took his leave.

At home, he removed his disguise and resumed his study. *Hitty's cooking will get a bypass, but the politicians will gain,* he said to himself. The early light of morning streaked through his tiny window before he stopped and went to bed.

Hitty was up early, intent on seeing Sadie before she left for the office.

The Internal Security personnel lived in Ward 10 about a mile from Hitty's Building. She strayed along the sidewalks and through the back streets until she reached Building 17, unit 19. Sadie opened the door and waved her to the table where a pot of tea and a plate of toast sat.

"What brings you out so early? My hankering for the office gang has fled. It's been so long since our transfer."

"In the neighborhood and decided to stop by." Hitty replied while pouring a cup of tea and helping herself to two slices of toast.

"Heh! She says," Sadie countered. "Tell me the real reason you're here."

"My mentoring duties bring me your way, and my present mentoree stretches my noggin to the limit."

"I have no experience in that arena, but I've added a bit in the security zone. You seized the best job years ago when we were neophytes."

"Our neophyte nights are swishing somewhere in the river Lethe, so I'll settle for a helping of security," Hitty replied.

"A sparse helping it will be. We check the residents in on arrival and make sure they don't loiter in the streets or anywhere else. The Labor Bureau may call us in when one of the workers is absent. The residents give us very little trouble. We're in charge of the rare public events that come our way.

"You may have heard our Head Honcho is coming to town. The buzz is making the rounds and meetings are scheduled nightly for this month."

"I heard, but another matter brought me your way. Security took a couple of young students to The Works recently. Do you know anything about the incident, Sadie?"

"No, some leeway is permitted to the local security force, but students are off limits. If you know who did the deed I can take care of it, Hitty."

"The incident has been rectified. No use to dredge up past abuses. However, I will keep your offer in mind."

"As you wish, but I'm here for you. You earned my gratitude when Swinne got the notion to do me in. What's the bore, Swinne been up to?"

"He's still at his games, I hear. He's a district educational administrator. Vexy is under his supervision and she teaches my pupil."

"He's not one of the students you were referring to, is he Hitty?"

"No, he isn't. The incident I referred to involved twin pupils of another Mentor, our dear Vexy. Odds are, Swinne had something to do with it, or we don't know our Swinne."

"I'll probe into it, Hitty, on the side."

"Follow your leanings, Sadie, but be careful how you go."

"I've learned a mite since our tussle with schemer Swinne, and minding my step is a habit." Sadie rose from her chair and said, "Keep in touch, Hitty. My early night at the office. Can't be late."

Back at home, Hitty reviewed their conversation and said to herself, *she didn't tell me everything about the security forces. Best not to know.*

<hr />

Brat got out of bed, took a shower, and dressed. *Hitty first, then the twins. The problem with Vexy? Too bad, she didn't remain an Earthie. She'd be a great politician. Come to think about it, she may have been one.*

The smell of food came to him as he entered Hitty's door. "Umm--bring it on. A plate or three will do."

"Pour your espresso, Brat, and fill a cup for me."

Brat sat and stared at her with a faraway look in his eyes. Hitty, restive under his gaze, said, "What's the matter lost your tongue?"

"I've been thinking, Hitty. The humans have codes of ethics. As far as I can tell, their practice is faulty, but they pitch them. We don't have any ethics. Why is that?"

"Why ask me, Brat. I'm a Mentor not a philosopher. If I were, I'd be down on the fourth level working at the quarry."

"Hitty, do you believe in goodness?"

"What do you mean by goodness, Brat?"

"It's like this. The humans have a code of ethics that are rules on how to be good. They teach that it's wrong to violate the rules, even though they do. I've read they can also change their behavior from bad to good and vice versa.

"So, what I mean by goodness is being kind, helpful, and caring. Somehow, the words resonate with my disposition."

"You are the strangest creature. When you say the words, I almost feel them. The residents here retain the same conduct fetched from their homeport. There's no such thing as good in Daganland. The climate in these districts squelches any bent towards it. HH makes certain of that."

"What age are you, Hitty."

"Whatever age I was on arrival is my age, Brat. Birthdays and age aren't relevant here. My hair has a touch of gray, so I'm middle-aged measured by the human standard."

"I'm nineteen years of age. I have a dim memory of someone shouting, "'Happy Birthday, Brat.'""

"What does age have to do with goodness, Brat?"
"Not much. Just a question on my mind lately, Hitty."

"Best to keep the questions under lock and key is my advice."

"Speaking of advice, Vexy is due home any night. Any counsel on surviving?"

"I suspect, Brat, Vexy has bigger fish than students on her mind after a month of whetting her appetite with Seminars. Delay your worries until she flops back into the pond."

"One more question and we'll close, Hitty. If we bring our behavior with us how come we didn't bring our casing with us?"

"You'll have to go down to the fourth level to ask the philosophers that question, Brat. I'm on the first level and fancy no other."

"If you happen to learn the answer, throw it my way. I'm off to the twins."

"You'll be the catcher of any dribs caught in my snare.

"Oh, Hitty, I forgot. Apples don't grow in the dark. Why are they so plentiful here?"

"You are an inquisitive fellow, Brat. Imported, that's why. Imported from the Earthlings. They're our biggest contributors in the edible department."

The twins were engaged in role-playing on Brat's entrance.

They had moved their desk into a corner to make room for their thespian activities.

"Welcome, Brat. Join us in a daily routine of an office. Hassel is taking us to an office next week to study the real thing. There's so much to learn, it quite squashes us." Luna said.

"Your enthusiasm for the squashes is on a par with your cramming lately."

"True, Brat. We do love it. Hassel says we are his most enthusiastic students."

"Enough self applause, Luna," Wim said.

"Have you any thoughts on the Vexy problem, Brat?"

"Hitty said to wait until she gets back. She may be whetting her appetite for higher elevations than the classroom."

"My thoughts are frozen, Brat, if Hitty said it," Wim replied.

Wim put their books aside and Brat helped to move the desk to its usual position.

"A new flavor from the specialty tea shop, Brat? I walked the entire way to get it expressly for you. My last pence."

"You will spoil me at this rate but my urgent errand claims attention?"

"Urgent, uhh—mind telling us the ins and outs of your errand?" Wim asked.

"I do mind. Be at ease, my friends, while I gather material for my class assignment."

"The word friend is never heard in these hallowed parts,

Brat. Watch yourself," Luna said.

"Look who's advising," Brat said and rose from his chair.

"Continue your play, my children. Study claims my attention."

A bit early for Polwin, Brat thought as he walked home. *Studies can wait. Think I'll drop into the bookshop.* Ten minutes later, he entered the four by four foot space. Books were mainly on rules and security issues. He chose a book, titled, Guardians of Your Security. He handed his pence to the ancient shopkeeper.

"Read, do you, youngster? Never learned myself. Been at this job awhile though I don't sell many books. Readers are scarce in these parts."

"Why are there no readers?"

"No books are written and the subjects are limited. Authors find the Gulag is their next stop," the shopkeeper said.

"Another pence for your information," Brat said, handing it to him. *My author fancies are kaput before I fancied any ,*he grumbled to himself. *HH is a miser and we are his coins.*

At home, he skimmed through the book on Daggie security. *Guardian is a fitting description. Reminds me of the financial wizards describing their jobs.*

He dressed in his grubby overalls, covered his hair with a matching hat, and went into the street. The crescent moon shown dimly and the streets were dark and empty.

He took a detour and soon found himself at the entrance to the elevators leading downwards. On exiting the elevator, he saw Building 313 on his right. He slipped inside and knocked on the door of unit 39.

A quavering voice came from the inside, "Who's there?"

"Brat. Seeznscin sent me." The door opened inch by inch and revealed a dusty face with bristly hair that stuck to his head like coiled springs.

"Come in youngster. A short visit we'll make of it, I'm right tired from wrestling with the sewer pipes."

"Polwin, short it will be. You know why I'm here, I gather."

"I do young fellow." He motioned him to the table and said, "A politician's life isn't all perks and preaching. A life of compromise and maneuvering in the crowded marketplace is what it is."

"How did you decide to be a politician Mr. Polwin?"

"It was this way, Brat. I was an idealistic young man. Politics called to me, I answered the calling, and began to orate at every opportunity. I was good at orating, Brat, none better. Soon there were large groups following me. It didn't hurt that I was handsome and a charmer. Scores of ladies adored me. The leaders of my party sought me out and encouraged me to run for office. In a word, I managed to become governor of a state, and national fame followed.

"It wasn't lost on me that party politics got dirty at times. However, my belief that I was working for the greater good of my country lessened any misgivings. As the years wore on, the misgivings disappeared, and I was keen for battle.

"The cutthroat arena became a Roman Coliseum where one lived or died politically. I was a gladiator fighting for my life, and I fought with no holds barred. I ascended to the presidency of my country, and whispers of treachery began circulating. The media picked upon it.

My methods of leading came under attack, and the accusations of foul play followed me wherever I went.

"The ruin of good men and women was laid at my door, and worse. I shrugged it off and charged my security detail to take care of the most vocal critics. They silenced the critics, but the whispers grew louder, and the people rose up.

"In short Brat, I was dethroned. The game was over, my supporters deserted me, and my life held little meaning. No regrets for me. I fought and I lost, that's all. Somewhere in the midst of combat, I lost the moral values of my youth. In an ironic sense, I came to the proper place. This place doesn't seem to have a moral code."

"An exciting tale, Mr. Polwin. Do you ever long for your past life."

"Not often, Brat. Brooding is forbidden. Work is doubled for one offence. For two offences, it's a sentence of four years on the fifth level. Three more years to go on the pipeline. I keep any pining to myself. Better men than me took over my country. If you wish further specifics on politics we can meet again next week."

"Mr. Polwin, you have given me insight into your affairs, and I'm grateful. The info is enough coupled with my studies. You have earned the pence."

They said good night, and Brat made his way home to study and to sleep.

Secrets

8

Hitty tidied her staclet when Brat had gone and went in search of Prye. She knocked on his door and waited for an answer. Behind her in the hallway, someone said, "You looking for Prye?"

Hitty whirled around and faced a figure dressed in a brown uniform. His dress and appearance blended. *Like my ginger bread cookies,* she thought. His dark brown hair in corkscrew curls fell to his shoulders and he looked at her with quizzical reddish brown eyes. He put his key in the lock and opened the door.

"Come in, I've been expecting you, Hitty. Sadie high- fived me."

She went in and explained her sleuthing task. "My trainee is a clever youth, brainy and cagey. I want you to follow him for a week and report to me on his activities."

While she talked, Prye kept nodding his head and said, "We're versed in secrecy, Hitty. Who's the most clever is the question. Let us seal our agreement on the pence for an expert sleuth."

When she took her leave an hour later, the contract was signed. Prye would begin his snooping the next night at two pence an hour.

Hah! Prye will out you, Brat, Hitty said to herself as she detoured home. *Why not trust me with your doings? I've grown fond of the peculiar chap, and fondness is frowned upon.*

⸻

Brat dropped in to the twins staclet with a gift of sweets. They shared a cup of tea then walked to class. About a block from the school, they caught a glimpse of a brown clad Daggie. He stood on the opposite side of the street in the doorway of a building observing them with a penetrating gaze.

A secret agent, Brat thought. *Better, be on watch.*

"I wonder why that fellow is hiding in the doorway, and staring at us," Luna said.

"Let's not get paranoid," Wim replied. "A worker on his lunch hour, probably."

"What do you think, Brat?" Luna asked.

"Wim is right, Luna. We need to plan for Vexy's grand entrance. A toady serving from each of us is due her."

"Her absence has been my bliss. To even think of her gives me the shudders," Luna said.

"Shudders aside, we will have to endure her presence. A tragic stage for your drama skills, no less."

"I'll do my best, Brat. Wim will push me off the stage if I forget my lines."

Hassel and Beterbe stood by the door of the classroom talking. They hastily separated on seeing the students enter the building. Hassel greeted them with a cheery wave, but his expression was somber. "Swinne is pleased with your progress," he said to them. "He claims bragging rights and broadcasts throughout the Ed department that his pupils are the best."

"Beterbe okay?" Brat asked.

"As of tonight he is. Vexy is to be here at our next class. We'll welcome her with a class party. Your contribution will be half a cake. Beterbe and I will supply the drinks. Any problems with funds? If so I can do the cake."

"No problems," Brat replied. "Luna can make it."

" Me?" Luna said. I don't....

Brat broke in with a signal to her. "I'll buy the ingredients for you."

"Your pence and my baking skills, Brat."

"No problem, Hassel. The best cake ever will be your," she said.

They traipsed out of the classroom and dawdled on the way home talking of Vexy's return.

"What a misfortune she wasn't recruited for a witch at one of the seminars," Luna said. "Be the very thing for her temperament."

"Her talents may propel her onwards and upwards. Let's not fret until we see in which direction she soars," Brat said.

"As long as she doesn't soar our way," Wim commented.

"About the cake," Luna said to Brat. "We're scheduled for an office observation. I'd better do the baking when I get home."

Brat gave her coins to cover the cost. She and Wim went into the grocery store and left him to his musings.

To Hitty's for brunch, then on to plan my date with a politico. Best to put the names in my cap and draw one.... His thoughts were interrupted by a glimpse of a head poking around the corner of a building.

Aha!, he said to himself. *Vexy in operation?* The head quickly withdrew as Brat came to a puzzled stop to mull over the possibilities.

Hitty was at the stove stirring a pot on his entrance. "Take a bowl of soup home with you. Your mental powers need a boost with all this study."

"I could use a boost, Hitty. On my way to class, and coming home, a weird figure appeared to be tailing me. Why would anyone follow me? Any ideas?

She stirred the pot vigorously and said, "Don't know, Brat. I'll sift through my quick-wits for you. You're on high alert for Vexy's return. Must be your nerves?"

"Nerves, Hitty? I expect better from a quick-wit than drivel."

"Forget it, and be alert, Brat. If it happens again, the talk will be on a less driveling plane"

They discussed his plans for observing a politician, then Brat said goodnight. "Don't forget your soup," Hitty said. He trudged home with the soup and his thoughts.

Funny. Hitty didn't want to talk about my experience with the tail or what I think was a tail.

At home, he plotted out his political operation, then he chose ten names from the roster given to him by Hassel. He closed his eyes and put his finger on a name.

Hope it's one close to the Daggies. I don't like the plane trips. He opened his eyes and read the name, Astira Dogmihyde.

A woman in the middle of North America. A junket of an hour or two.

I need a break and Kruknsak could use his pence a mite early, Brat thought. He dressed in his seedy overalls, put the matching hat on, and went out the back way. Kruknsak opened the door to his knock, and Brat entered.

"Welcome to my home, young Brat," he said. "Not the comforts of my former one but these suit me. My wants are scant."

"Our wants are somewhat squashed by our locale, Mr. Kruknsak. I brought your pence and an extra month's lot. I may be going here and there for awhile."

"Best not to inquire where your goings are, young Brat?"

"Correct, Mr. Kruknsak. Goings are silent events."

"Farewell then, young Brat. On many occasions, I had the chance to befriend youngsters and refused their pleas. It might have been my lot to have met someone like you. Consequently, this place may have been missing one member."

"It was our lot meet here, Mr. Kruknsak. Drink a malt to toast the occasion." Brat said goodbye and left the old man to his musings.

Once in the street, he walked to the corner and scrutinized the surroundings. Seeing no one, he ran to the back alley and made his way home. Inside, he viewed the street from his pint-sized window and saw a brown clad figure gazing at the building's entrance.

Good thing I go in disguise. My wits and yours will have a workout before I'm through with you, *Mr. Brown,* he said to himself. *What to do? To do or not to do is the question. Risky either way. Here goes.*

He dressed in a navy blue uniform, a navy blue cap, pasted his mustache on his upper lip, and went out the back. The street was emptied of pedestrians and devoid of moonlight. He strolled to the end of the building, felt his way to the front corner lit by the fiery glow of the furnaces, and peered at the brown clad figure leaning against the building.

"Hello there," Brat said, and walked closer. The startled figure turned and looked at Brat's blue uniform.

"Getting a bit of the evening air," he replied in a strangled voice.

Brat played along, "Aren't you from the ...what division is that?"

A fleeting look of dismay covered the brown clad Daggie's face. He replied in a low tone, "The Internal Division of Security."

"I'm with the Special Ops," Brat said. "You must be working late."

"No. shift is over. The night air is refreshing before dinner."

"The air it is then, a topping night to you," Brat said and walked in the direction of a neighboring building.

He then went through the back alley to his staclet and sat at the table in thought. *Why am I under scrutiny and who is it? Vexy? She's had enough trouble with students. Swinne? He dare not mess with students after the debacle with the twins. Think another jog to Hitty's is on order before the alluring Ms. Dogmihyde wins my attention.*

Brat mapped out his route to the politico's district and spent two hours studying her political activities. *No wonder she wants to be a partaker of partisan spoils. She's like Vexy, a natural born actor.*

Soon after, he knocked on Hitty's door. The door opened to a puzzled, "Back again, Brat? Can't stay at home for a night?"

"Right, Hitty. I miss you too much. Got a possible set-up to run by you."

"Run it by fast, Brat. I'm busy with my beauty routine this hour of the night."

"A sit and a cup of tea are required for the telling, or more likely tailing. And while we're at it, what is your beauty routine?"

"None of your business. Get to the telling."

He recited his experience with the brown clad figure and watched her facial expression. She attempted to turn her face from his gaze, but he followed her movements to keep her face in view.

"It must be your imagination, Brat. Why would anyone want to bag you in their net?" She asked with a flushed face.

"That's what I'm trying to find out, Hitty. You're savvy in matters involving security. Hints are often thrown my way."

"Hints are one thing and knowing is another. Who's dumb enough to let a nineteen year old find him out?"

"Him, Hitty? I didn't say anything about a Him." She sipped her tea for a moment and then said in a stifled tone, "Most tails are male, Brat."

"Maybe so, but she, or he, wears a brown uniform, so I thought it might be a female."

"Go on home, Brat, if you happen to see the figure again. Come tell me."

"For certain. The tail will be trapped, Hitty."

*Aha...*Brat said to himself as he scurried home, *Got you, Hitty. Thought you could fool me. Curiosity came calling and you fed the creature.*

An hour after Brat left, Hitty zipped to Prye's in a huff. He opened the door to her furious red face.

She burst out, "You're a smart PI? So smart as to be unmasked on your first tailing."

His brows drew together. "What do you mean, Hitty? I'm doing what you told me to do. I didn't catch sight of the target tonight. I've only glimpsed him once."

"Have you met anyone that seems a little strange on your prowling."

"Not really. I met a fellow on security patrol earlier tonight. He seemed ordinary enough."

"You better be on close watch and report to me tomorrow night. Keep undercover. Don't let him see you and don't wear your uniform."

"No way will he see me, Hitty," he said, his face glowing a shade redder.

She took her leave and returned home uneasy and mystified. As she entered the building, Bitsy came to mind. *Two heads are better than one; she might have a slant on my operation.*

"Why come to me, Hitty? I barely know Prye, and that's from hearsay," Bitsy said. "Whoever seeks his service has a close mouth in these precincts. No one tells me their grievances." She scanned the empty hallway and said, "Come in."

Hitty sat and studied her teacup, as if she could find answers in the tea leaves, and then said, "If Prye is detected by the one he's following, what then?"

"Don't know, Hitty. I expect it's best to sack Prye."

"You're probably right, Bitsy. Two more days will end the play."

"Keep the date open and sack the gimp. Best for him and you."

"My ears are tuned to your song. I'll be in touch," Hitty

Brat slept and dreamed of beings in luminous costumes.

Where did they came from. No beings like that in the Daggie vicinity, he mumbled to himself next morning. His thoughts turned again to Vexy as he prepared his notes for Hassel.

He walked into class trailed by two nervous twins with the half cake. They sandwiched him between them so closely during their presentation that he began to feel a smothering sensation.

"Move over you two," he whispered, "Vexy won't eat you in class."

Hassel interrupted the twins presentation, "Vexy got back yester night and has some pleasing news for us."

"Pleasing news?" Brat said, still pressed by the twins on each side of him. "She's going to another planet, Hassel?"

He laughed and said, "I don't think so, Brat. Let's get the bash ready."

A noise in the corridor alerted them to Vexy's entrance.

She greeted them with a smile. "My pets, how I've missed you. Your welcome overwhelms me."

She chattered non-stop while the drinks and cake were being served, leaving Brat and the twins to sigh in relief. "Such delicious cake. You must give me the recipe, Luna. Who knew you had such talents. Office management too, Hassel tells me"

"Brat, I will sorely miss our sessions..."

"Vexy, you aren't leaving us? How could you do this to us?" Brat interrupted in a forlorn tone.

The twins stared at him with wide eyes, and then Vexy said cheerfully. "No tears allowed Brat. Hassel is an able teacher, not on my level, but you and the twins will adapt to him."

"We wish you well wherever you go, Vexy. Where are you going?" Brat asked.

"One of the directors of the Internal Security Division in one of my seminars invited me to apply for a post. I did and the letter of acceptance came early tonight."

"When do we have to give you to the noble service?" Luna asked with her eyes on Brat.

"Next week and cut the noble. The office staff and students will be given notice. I will present my three pets and Hassel a first showing of my uniform."

"Oh joy, what a break, "Luna said on their way home." She can show off all she wants, but does it have to be on our stage? To think I wasted energy on her, worrying myself to pieces. "

"Don't throw your caution in the bin yet. Vexy is a power climber. We may hear from her again." Brat said.

"My fingers are crossed." She took Wim's hand and crossed his fingers. "We're both fervent wishers that it's the last of her."

"Fervent it is," Wim said, "with red-hot wishes" "We'll be on guard and wishes won't hurt," Brat replied.

Affairs of State

9

Better find the lurker and move in on him. Brat centered his thoughts on Prye and kept near to the buildings. He spotted him as he neared his building. Prye stood in the moonlight with a hand to his forehead peering through Brat's window. His brown uniform was gone, but his long hair and his posture at the window gave him away.

"Looking for me?" Brat asked. Prye spun around and stammered. "No, no. Inspecting the window. It looked broken from the street. I guess it was the cast of the moonlight."

"Would you like to come in for a cup of tea?" Brat asked. "A reward is a small matter for a considerate fellow like you."

Prye took a step backwards as if to take flight and then stopped. He glanced up and down the street, looked at Brat, and said. "That's a welcome treat. Lead me in.

Once inside, he said, "I'm Castur, and your name?"

"I'm Brat, a student at the Swinne academy."

"A privileged someone?"

"Can't say, Castur," Brat said. "Hitty is my Mentor. Maybe you know her."

Prye moved his eyes from side to side to avoid his gaze, lowered his head, and said, "Can't say I do."

"I passed your staclet a night or two ago and saw her go into your building."

"What building was that?"

"Building 71."

Prye sat quietly a moment, took a sip of tea, and then looked at Brat. "No use to lie. I'll 'fess up and beg mercy, on account of you're not in a position to snitch. Everybody hides something."

"Correct. Castur, or is it Prye?"

"Prye, it is. And you are actually, Brat?"

"I'm Brat. You're Hitty's PI. Why does she want you to follow me?"

"Don't know why. Never ask my clients. I do the job I'm given."

"If you poke about, I'll double the pence she's paying you."

"You have a deal, Brat. Hitty said you were clever. How did you out me?"

"Wasn't easy, Prye," Brat said, and grinned at him. "I noticed your shadow one night. I advise you to detect from safer areas than corners and doorways."

"Advice well taken. When do we begin this deal of ours?"

"No better time than the present. What is Hitty rate?"

"Two pence an hour, and little enough for the harried life I lead."

"Three pence and a bonus of another three if you get the info for me?"

"Will do, Brat," he said as he rose and made for the door.

<hr />

Time to do a little advance scouting of my own, Brat thought. He packed a light bag and retrieved his map of Ms. Dogmihyde's territory. She lived in a northeast coastal city of North America. *A two-hour trip. Best to check it out by the universal positioning system.*

He left by the back way and went to the educational building. The device was mounted on a desk in the reference section of the library. After getting his flight pattern adjusted, he marked the route on his map and started to leave for home.

Then a thought came to mind. He stopped and went back to view the GPS. *Might as well see where Synlan is while I'm here.* He mapped the city, the route to it, and as he exited the library muttered to himself, *a four hour roundtrip to view the political ploys of a public servant, and no plane. I'm tired already.*

He hitched his backpack on, fastened the clasps of his tunic, and began his journey. He alighted on the verandah of Ms. Dogmihyde's home two hours later. The noise of laughter drifted to him through the open door, and Brat saw a large gathering in full swing. He stepped into the reception area and gazed at the immense room lit up by pendant chandeliers.

People in evening clothes were milling about with drinks in their hands while white coated waiters were passing trays of food. Groups of people were gathered in huddles. He spotted Ms. Dogmihyde moving among the guests with a sparkling smile. She stopped to talk with a group engaged in conversation.

Brat slipped into the group and looked her over. *Another Vexy? What's with this feminine copy? The Daggies don't need any more Vexy's.*

Her raven hair was bound into a top knot and her diamond earrings glittered in harmony with the chandeliers. Her slender green suited figure assumed an assertive stance and she spoke in a firm persuasive voice.

"The people of my state deserve a representative who will be committed to their interests. I am that person. If you will support me in this election, you won't be forgotten."

A man in a gray suit said, "The wife and I are considering a switch to your candidacy. My business is going under from the taxes. What is your stand on tax issues?"

"I am for less taxes, period. Personal and business taxes are out of control in this state. We will work to lessen their impact. Important issues are to be discussed at a town meeting. I want to see you there."

She returned to mingling, and Brat mingled too.

Kruknsak's kind of scene, he thought as he walked among them and listened to the dialogue about yachts and leisure activities.

A woman spoke from a podium at the back of the room, and the guests quieted.

"We extend our thanks to each of you for your support. Your gifts are the vital link to winning this election, and win we will. And now a break in the fund pitch. Please make your way to the dining room. Takachek manages the funds in case any extras are leftover, and I don't mean food."

Brat sped to the food while the guests were laughing and seating themselves. He swiped a plate, slid under the table, and waited.

When the guests were distracted by the serving staff, he emerged and nicked food from two of the plates. *Braying and eating. Not much braying where I come from, but Daggies make up for it by eating,* Brat thought.

I think I've heard and seen enough of this fund raising gala, he said to himself an hour later.

He arrived home in the late hours of the night, collapsed on the bed, and fell asleep wrapped in his tunic.

Earlier in the night, Hitty had gone to see Prye to quiz him on his night's sleuthing.

"Well?" she snapped. "My pence are in the balance. Any news?"

"No fooling you, Hitty. Your target seems to go about his routine of class and study with no quirky habits."

"Brat doesn't fool me either. He's too smart for you. Your pence tonight and we'll end this farce of snooping?"

"Fair enough, Hitty. I opine the young Daggie is on the lookout for snoopers. Best to ask him why he goes prowling, if he does."

"Are you saying I can't have a fun-fest at Brat's expense?"

"No, the fun-fest is likely to be at your expense if you continue with this PI stuff. The young fellow knows how to outwit you."

"I did so look forward to getting the best of Brat, but admitting defeat is an option. I'll give in and declare him the winner of this round."

"Hitty, why did you hire me for this task?"

"For a fun-fest, Prye. Enough said?"

"Your words lack meaning, but as you say, enough."

Hitty went home in a grumpy mood, made tea, and sat debating the question of how to approach Brat. *His evasive tactics aren't attuned to my mentoring duties,* she thought. *A long chat is in the offing.*

When she had cleaned the kitchen after breakfast, she decided to visit Sadie again. *My flop in the nosey direction requires an audience.*

She sat on the settee and read her book on humans until the security shift ended. Then she traipsed to Sadie's some time later and reviewed Prye's botched case with her. Brat's name was not mentioned.

"Not much to say, Hitty. Prye makes a pence or two extra, but he doesn't guarantee results."

"It was on my mind and I wanted to run it by you. Any news on the Swinne incident?"

"In fact, there is. The rumor is swirling that he and Vexy teamed to set-up two students and one of the office assistants."

"It's true all right," Hitty said. "Their plot was foiled. The students are in class, and the assistant back at his post. If the plot becomes known in the higher circles, Vexy and Swinne will take a nosedive to the lower fifth floor. Mining for coal and copper is their proper forte."

"Let's see how the two meet their fates," Sadie said. "Vexy is being assigned to the special security detail. If she comes into my unit, my rank will insulates me somewhat. Watching my back while she schemes will get tiresome."

Hittie rose from the table and set her cup on the countertop. She puckered her lips and said, "I suspect she won't be in a mood to practice her wily schemes any time soon.
The arrival of our Head Honcho is a distraction in the near term."

"Right, Hitty. The talk centers on him every night. I'll keep you posted if you wish."

"Do that, Sadie," Hitty said on exit.

Brat slept and dreamed of luminous beings dressed in pale green fabric. Hair of a fine golden or brown texture fell in ringlets around pale faces and black ringlets framed bronzed faces. They resembled humans in outline, but a radiant beauty marked their forms.

The beings were walking down a street lit by the sun and Brat flinched in his sleep from the dazzling light. An open green space bordered the street and descended to a river.

They went up white glistening steps and entered a marble building. A corridor led them into a large room where an older individual dressed in clothes of a sunlit gold stood at a podium. Behind him, a large chart filled with mathematical symbols, seemed familiar to Brat.

He awoke and rose to sit by the window to ponder on his dream.

He sat for an hour and went back to bed. *No sense to it,* he said to himself and fell asleep again.

Near twilight, tired of flailing about in restless sleep, he got out of bed, brewed coffee, and sat fretting over the dream.

Useless, he said to himself. *Hitty had better interpret this one. What's a Mentor for?*

"What are you doing here so early? Can't you give me time to dress?" Hitty said, as he walked in without knocking.

"Dress or no dress, you have to help me. Your mentoring abilities are on the line."

"Dress, I will. Go outside and stare at the moon for ten minutes and come in like a polite Daggie."

"Didn't know there were any. Polite is not our strong suit."

"Never mind. Move yourself to the hallway, if not to the moon."

Hitty washed and dressed, and then motioned to Brat, busy pacing the hallway, to come in.

"What's the matter with you, Brat? You look like you've seen a ghost. Or is there a Daggie ghost?"

"This dream filching my sleep is nagging me."

He relayed the details of the two episodes and said, "You're my Mentor so give me an explanation."

"An explanation, Brat?" she said in an aggrieved tone. "I have no idea what your dream means. Why ask me? I'm not a seer."

"Your vast experience, Hitty. A Mentor of talent like you must hear of mystifying experiences."

"I've never mentored anyone like you, Brat, so there goes your theory of me."

"Aside from my dreams, there's the mystery of the furtive watcher whom I saw near my unit last night. What do you make of that?"

"A watcher, Brat? Someone in your building may be his target. Why do you think it's you?" she said with a flushed face.

She got up, went to the stove, and started whipping eggs into an omelet.

"If you see him again, come tell me."

"You said him. I'm getting suspicious of you, Hitty," Brat replied. "Are you on the level with me?" "You don't always share your activities with me, and, yes, I am curious as to why you don't. Take the coins. Where exactly did you get them?"

"Gee-oh, Hitty, I've already told you where— remember?"

"I thought you were funning at my expense. And what's with the nightly prowling at the pub with Daggie workers?"

"It's part of my studies. Do you have to know every little thing?"

"I do if you don't mind."

"Some things remain unsaid. Pacify yourself with a cup of espresso."

While they ate, he brought her up to date on his visit to Ms. Dogmihyde. "She looks like a Vexy, glossy and ambitious. Though there's an aura about her, which hints of honesty, she may be on the take. Whatever, I hope she retains the aura."

"Hopes are never amiss. You speak as if a budding sympathy for the humans is taking root. Not allowed, you know."

"The fault of Kruknsak Sr., I guess. Humans are such simpletons. Elicits the tender side of me."

"Forget the humans and the tender side. A hearty breakfast will toss the sympathy from your system, or a Daggie Tosser will do it for you in the coal pits.

"You sway me, Hitty, with your warning.

On his way out, he said, "No ideas on the dreams, huh?"

"None, Brat, but when you spoke, an image came to mind, a picture of a white house glistening in the sun. My muse has a standing invitation, and her ideas are at your disposal on your next stopover."

"I'll be here after class."

"You might give me a night or two."

"After class, Hitty."

At home, Brat took his tome on the human world to the kitchen and spread it open on the table. He thumbed to the section on agriculture and its products. A colorful page on fast food caught his eye, and he read for an hour before leaving for class.

Luna and Wim came down the steps as he approached their building. Both met him with a smile and a cheerful hello. He beckoned to them without a return greeting and whispered, "Safest not to speak to each other in the street."

"Your tip is obeyed, Brat," Wim said.

On walking into the classroom, they were unsettled to see Swinne sitting at the desk with Hassel.

"We have a visitor, tonight," Hassel said and looked at them with upraised eyebrows. "Mr. Swinne is so pleased with your progress he agreed to join us tonight."

The twins and Brat exchanged glances, muffled their groans, and sat down.

Mr. Swinne settled himself in a chair, crossed his arms, and observed their narration.

Nervous, Luna and Wim began stammering out their presentation. As they proceeded their enthusiasm for the subject triumphed. Swinne's presence was only a blurred shape as they burbled on office management.

Brat recited the details of his reading assignment and his political observations in a neutral voice. Then he asked Mr. Swinne for any helpful comments.

"No comments needed, Brat. Superior instructors make superior students. Your performance honors me."

He rose and went to his office leaving the four of them to wipe their brows in relief.

"Hassel, I'm rather fond of this assignment, but what's it for? Vexy didn't tell me." Brat said.

"You are slated to head the intake department for the humans at the end of your studies, Brat. I thought you knew."

"First time I've heard of it. What are the most important points in my studies, Hassel?"

"The behavioral traits, pros and cons, of humans. You will learn the procedures of admission later."

"I can do that, Hassel. An inquiry into human customs and conduct has been stimulating to say the least."

"You will begin the office studies next year, Brat."

Think Selnby needs a consult, Brat said to himself as he parted from the twins and walked to Hitty's.

* * *

"Now, Hitty, you're in for it. So splutter your views on my dream predicament."

She poured two cups of tea, gave one to him, and then sat down at the table. "You are the most trying pupil, Brat. A handful of Daggies have passed through my door, but never one like you."

"Never mind, Hitty. Cough up your ruminations. I've got places to go."

"I don't have an answer for your dreams, Brat. I don't have one for my fleeting image of a white house. What I do have is a tale that happened years ago. May be a help in explaining the bright light around the Earthlings."

"I'm listening. See the tips of my perky ears."

"I caught the end of the affair, and it was strange, even by Daggie standards. One night, I was tending to my own business when an awful roar in the street drew me to the window.

"Groups of Daggies were marching in rows with their arms waving back and forth and shouting silly verses. I ran outside to ask the why of the hullabaloo.

"I tagged a Daggie who said in a gleeful voice, "'We're having fun with two weird looking creatures perched on the steps of the security building.'"

"I ran to the building and saw two humans sitting within a glowing light so intense its rays streamed in every direction. A young boy and a girl, a bit younger than you, clung closely to each other. I could see they were frightened. Then, suddenly two huge figures appeared, picked up the two of them, and disappeared.

"All the Daggies moved backwards and fell on top of each other when the two huge figures appeared. Then everyone sped off home without a word, and I wasn't far behind them."

"I do like your story, Hitty. I can't fathom how it fits in with my dreams. They were beings from the Supreme Honcho?"

"I suppose they were. It tallies with the incident. When you said the humans were surrounded by a light, I connected the two events. The lights appear to be similar."

"I'll compute the matter in my noodle a night or two and print out the solution, if any."

"Don't forget to clue me in with your solution. I'll be waiting with tuned ears."

"I'll share the swag, Hitty.

Sampling the Human World

10

Brat changed into his gritty overalls, covered his hair with a cap, and sneaked out the back entrance. He skulked through the alleys and found Selnby at home.

The Daggie who opened the door was less than three feet tall with shaggy brown hair and eyes of an orange hue.

"Kruknsak warned me that you were a persistent young fellow," he said and smiled at Brat.

"A student's life has its own problem. It's my lot to beg info from every available source."

"A cup of tea is a warm-up for such," Selnby motioned towards the table.

Brat scanned the room, and said, "Seems we all have the same amount of space and furnishings. Do you know the reason for it, Mr. Selnby?"

"Don't question—don't ask, Brat. A gift to us masses, I reckon."

"Has your stay in these parts been a long one, Mr. Selnby?"

"Long enough to forget my former haunts and to wonder how I got here. Mostly the nights are taken up with work and the days with sleep. The lees of remembrance are draining from me."

"Quite poetic. Did you ever consider being a poet, Mr. Selnby?"

"I did when I was a boy. I entered finance on graduating from college, and the dream slipped away."

"Your practice in the field of finance was extensive?"

"Indeed, Brat. A career that spanned forty years. I rose to be head of a large financial empire. In the process, I forgot all the teachings of my childhood. Power was my twenty-four hour companion, pushing me to ever-greater heights. And the heights grew steeper with financial manipulations as the summit's prize."

"Childhood, Mr. Selnby? Your teachings?"

"My teachings on honesty and trust, Brat. I faulted them as concepts developed to restrain the weak. They didn't apply to the strong ones of the world like me."

"The manipulations? Can you explain them in a brief summary?"

"To lend and borrow money is a human tradition. However, I conspired with others throughout the international markets to rack up gains of billions of dollars. We did it by insider tips and rigging the scales that measure the rates for lending purposes. The perilous slope for my descent was in the making from my first job. I didn't stent with the building materials, and when the day of reckoning came, as it does in the human world, I woke up here."

"Mr. Selnby, your tips are worthy ones. The info will be useful in developing policies for our Intake Department. If you ever stop in my neighborhood, come by for a chat."

"Nay, Brat. Work and sleep with a bite to eat is all I'm good for these nights."

⚬⚬⚬

Wonder why the teachings on ethics are so violated in the human world? Brat thought, as he zigzagged home.

He changed clothes, secured his backpack, and then began his journey to the politician's home.

He set down on a graveled driveway and walked up to the front entrance. The house was dimly lit and the door was unlocked. He entered and wandered through the empty rooms.

He found a telephone on a desk and punched an answering machine. *Good thing I learned about phones and gadgets,* he thought while listening to the message, 'At headquarters, come on down.'

How am I to come on down? He looked for a phone number and found it in an appointment diary. He dialed the number, and someone said, "Hello."

"Directions, please," Brat said, in a good imitation of a human's voice.

The directions written, Brat began his walk to the headquarters building. Halfway there, he spied a yellow arch and the sign reading, McDonald's. *Fast food is calling me and I must answer,* he thought, as he made a beeline inside.

He stood and eyed the crowded interior and the line of people waiting to give their order. Two men near him were talking about a horse race. "Come along with me to the race, Carl. Shifty is ten to one and he's bound to win."

"Not this one, Ranse," the man replied, "Gotta get home to the wife,"

A horse race? A shifty horse race? Brat thought.

He noticed a man and woman sitting at a table with two small youngsters. Fascinated, he moved closer. Suddenly, the younger child caught sight of Brat and began laughing. He pointed towards him and slid from his chair to the floor.

The father grabbed the child who started crying. "What's the matter with you, Nate?" The child tried to wriggle from his father's hands. "Want to see the boy," he sniffed loudly. "No," his mother said, and lifted him onto her lap.

Brat moved into the crowd where the child couldn't see him, and watched as the orders were given and then received. *How to do this?* He looked over the counter and saw trays of food. *For me, one hamburger, a french fry and a drink.* When the workers were busy with the orders he hopped across the counter and put the fries and hamburger underneath his tunic.

Going to the drink machine, he stuck a small cup under the Pepsi sign. He pushed the button, picked up the filled cup, and went outside. He chose a back table that lay in shadows and began eating. *Tasty*, he said to himself, as he bit into the hamburger, *but not up to Hitty's standards.*

If the people who came and went through the doors saw a pair of phantom hands holding a hamburger and fries, Brat didn't notice. The double takes and quick getaways were ignored in his preoccupation with eating.

As he finished his meal, the man who had mentioned the horse race appeared and walked to a car. *Might as well find out what a shifty horse and a race is,* Brat thought, and followed the man, Ranse, into the car.

He settled in the front seat and watched Ranse fasten a belt around himself. *What's with the belt?*

Intent on his driving the man didn't notice a pair of hands sliding the belt on in the opposite seat. After five minutes or so Ranse glanced at the seat and said, "Almost feels like Junie is with me."

Ten minutes passed, and then they were in a large space filled with cars. Ranse parked the car, got out, and walked towards the racing stands with Brat by his side. He went to a window and bought a ticket." Give me sixty on the nose for Shifty."

Brat watched him while the mostly male crowd jostled their way to the window to buy a ticket. He inched his arm through the window and took a ticket. He followed Ranse to a front row of seats and spotted the horses in a horizontal line behind gates. Brat stared in astonishment at the figures seated on the backs of the horses.

Ranse said to a woman beside him, "I put sixty on Shifty. He better win."

"Which one is he?" the woman asked.

"Number six, second from the left, the black beauty."

Brat, mystified by the riders, glanced at the black horse. *Shifty must have a tough life,* he thought, *having to carry humans on his back.* He heard a bell ringing, and then someone yelled, "They're off."

All at once, the gates popped open and the horses bolted through. Brat sprang to the fence to get a better look and located Shifty, fifth from the lead. *Can't have that,* he said to himself.

He caught Shifty as he rounded the curve to home. He landed on his back, and the horse neighed in a high-pitched scream. Shifty ran past the other horses, past the stands, jumped the fence, and continued his frantic pace. He stopped when Brat got off to go in search of Ranse and his car.

Back at the grandstand, the stewards were in a huddle. They were at the head scratching stage when the jockey rode Shifty onto the racetrack. Shifty was declared the winner and everyone dispersed, including Ranse.

Brat found him at the payout window ecstatically babbling "Junie's two dozen roses...." He took the money handed to him, counted it, and put it in his billfold.

Brat inspected the office and the paper notes given to the winners. He saw an open cash register underneath the window. He laid his ticket on the counter, reached inside, and withdrew five of the notes from the drawer. *Pay for my ticket with the sixth note,* he thought.

By this time, Ranse was outside heading for his car. Brat took the notes, zipped toward the parking lot, and buckled himself into the seat. Ranse, still elated, squealed his tires, drove recklessly, and hummed a tune to Junie.

When Brat caught sight of the yellow arch, he left the car. He paused to look at his directions to the political headquarters. He then resumed walking towards it but halted halfway there. *Do I need more info on Ms. Dogmihyde? Think not, I'm not feeling so well. Must be the fast food and the jiggling from Shifty.* He scanned his map and headed for home.

━━━⋅⋅⋅

Brat stopped off to buy antacids at the neighborhood grocery, then went home, and staggered into bed. *No more of the fast food for me,* he thought, as he sank into sleep and dreamed of the luminous beings in green clothes. He walked up the steps of the marble building with them and entered the classroom. He sat in the second row facing the podium. The Instructor, watching the students enter and take their seat, said, "Back already, Brad?"

He awakened abruptly from the dream, threw the bedclothes off, and went to put the teapot on. *McDon-*

ald's fallout? Can't hire a PI for this, he said to himself as he puzzled over the dream.

He dressed in his blue uniform, stashed his dollar bills in the nook with his coins, and went out the back way. Soon after, he knocked on Prye's door. "What are you doing here, Brat? I expected you last night."

"To quote an Earthie poet, 'the best laid schemes....'" But now for your answer to my query about Hitty."

"Not much to tell. Hitty did it to best you, a fun-fest, she said."

"Hitty doesn't like to be topped by anyone. This extra coin is for your efforts. Let us end this play. Mind where you snoop, Prye."

"I'll be cagey in my snooping. Your lesson is stuck in the old bean. "

At home, Brat put on his regular clothes and knocked on Hitty's door a short time later.

"Are you moving in any time soon, Brat? Visiting can be cut considerably if you do."

"If anything is cut, Hitty, it won't be my visits. How is the fun-fest going?"

"Fun-fest? You've been sneaking behind my back, Brat," she replied in her most acerbic tone. "You try my nerves dreadfully."

"Try this then," he said. "Prye required a lesson before he landed on the fifth floor. Being merciful, I exposed the holes in his after hours roving."

"We'll forget the whole embarrassing affair. I can't win with you. Tell me the latest in your episodic roving."

"Breakfast first, if you don't mind." Hitty prepared the food while Ms. Dogmihyde, and the foray into fast food, got a thorough airing. He skipped the horse race and said, "There it is, my latest, Hitty. What about you? Any reports on the Big Cheese unfurling?"

"News from the lofty heights goes well with cappuccino, and it's your turn to make it."

"What a luxury!" she said a few minutes later. She took a sip and then said, "The latest rumor—Special Security will be here tomorrow night to oversee the planning committee. News is rationed in the Big Cheese department, Brat. HH tends to operate in the blackout mode."

"Wonder how Vexy is responding to the special security news," Brat said.

"If I know my Vexy, she's planning her chance of attracting attention from the Big Cheese. HH isn't known for catering to competition in the attention arena. On guard is the watch word."

"Suits me, Hitty. The politicians and the fast food wrung me dry, last night. My dream squeezed out any residues." He swallowed the last drops of his espresso and said, "It's time I tottered home to my books and class session."

"Brat and the twins entered the classroom and saw a vision in blue and black. Vexy, talking to Hassel, twirled in her new blue uniform and gleaming knee- high black boots. She flashed them a wide smile. "My pets," she said, "I have something for you."

She rummaged in her new shiny briefcase. "An invitation to visit my office." She handed each an engraved card. "I must be off, but be sure to stop in with Hassel, next week night. A class assignment."

She withdrew with a flourish and a backward wave. They looked at Hassel and groaned.

"I know, I know," he said. "We'll visit and make it short. She's posted to the local internal division. It's not far from here. You might as well get an introduction to its workings."

"A cup of green tea might comfort us at this sad hour," Brat said as they made their way home. "Stop in, and I'll brew a pot for us."

"How do you afford these luxuries, Brat? Between us we can only eke out a few pence for the lowly thing called tea and a home baked sweet," Luna said while they sat enjoying the special tea and buttered toast.

"Leave unasked, Luna, and enjoy the pricy offering is my advice."

"Wim and I have no yearning for another round with the coal stokers, Brat."

"I'll take the rounds for us if the occasion arises. Let us drink to the occasion never arising," he replied with lifted cup.

"Vexy is ambitious, and she has the very place to exercise her feelers. She will do herself in, but not by us. We're small fry," Brat said.

"These small fry never want to see Vexy again," Luna said on leave taking. "Wim and I have a week's posting to an office coming soon. And you, Brat, what are you doing these nights?"

"Enough for you to know that Hitty covets my presence and the Earthies summon me for an evening or two," he replied in a vague tone.

What dreams may come

11

After the twins went home, Brat sat pondering his next move. *Young Kruknsak is my target. Where do I find him?* He pulled a map of North America from beneath a stack of papers on his desk. He located New York City and the Sloane Building in midtown Manhattan.

After a jaunt to the library to program his route, he was set for the journey. At home, he packed a light bag with the dollars and a snack. He sneaked through the back ways in his tunic and took his flight.

He alighted at the Sloane Building. He went in and read the roster of names on a wall plaque. Kruknsak Jr. was near the bottom. It was nearing 5 am, and the dawn light was brightening.

An hour later, he spied Ole Sloane emerging from a vehicle. He entered the building and went into an elevator. Five minutes passed and his target came in. "Pssst... Kruknsak Jr.," Brat hissed.

The man stopped, petrified, his feet frozen to the floor. "Not again," he stammered with a whimper. "I did what you told me to. I'm a junior partner in the real estate division. I'm a nervous wreck from our last discussion."

"Don't fear, able son. No harm is intended. I'm checking for your father's sake. The news of your success will hearten him considerably.

"My job is going well, and Ole Sloane has taken a personal interest in me. I won't disappoint him, or Father," Kruknsak Jr. responded in a shaky voice.

"This visit may be the last if we can close another task today," Brat said.

Something like a sob slipped from Kruknsak Jr., but he said, "What task?"

A woman in a brown suit walking toward an escalator looked at Kruknsak and said, "Feeling under the weather this morning, Kruky?"

"No, Jacee," he said. "A call home, I'll be in the office in ten minutes."

Brat pulled the dollars from his backpack and said, "Two more pounds of the copper coins. Can you complete the task today?"

"Give me a couple of hours. My friend, Carson, will mint and send them by swift airfreight. I'm a partner in his firm. My father will be pleased at the news."

By this time, Kruknsak Jr. had regained his composure and spoke in a less fearful voice. The employees who were entering the building viewed him with curious head turnings.

His friend answered his ring, and the deal was finalized. "Three pounds... what is your name anyway?"

"I'm Brat. It's best to forget me."

"Forget you? If I told anyone about meeting you, I'd likely end up in the booby hatch. I have to get to the office. I'll meet you here in the lobby at 10 am."

"Is there a place to sleep in these digs?" Brat asked. "On the tenth floor. Turn left when you get off the elevator. The first door leads into an empty conference room."

Brat made a beeline for the elevator and was soon snoozing in comfort on a plush cushion.

He awakened when he heard the door open. Footsteps came close and a woman's voice said. "Hmmm... that pillow is crushed." She bent to fluff it and felt a form beneath her hands. She straightened up and ran from the room. Brat slept another hour and returned to the lobby.

Kruknsak Jr. was pacing in circles. "Over-slept, did you? Here you are." He handed Brat three bundles. "Give Father my love and a pound of the coins."

"I will, Kruknsak Jr... For your benefit, research the source of the bright light that sometimes appears in my country. It's a light of protection for some of the Earthies."

"Earthie? Who's an Earthie?"

"A Daggie term, a short term for humans."

"Maybe it describes us, at that. Ole Sloane talks about church and light. I'll consult him."

Brat arrived home, crannied the coins, and shed his clothes.

He slept until nightfall, arose, and took a cool shower. The memory of the falling water while he was with Husslm came to mind. *The water...how does the water get here? The purview of Hitty.*

⚞⚞⚞⚞⚞⚞⚞

His shower finished, he dressed, and speeded off to find answers to his question. "Here you are Hitty. I saw water in the air when I visited the Earthies. The air has no water here. Where does it come from? "

"Water here, Brat? For a clever fellow, you do ask simple questions. From the subterranean depths, that's where. Wells and cisterns hold the surface water that we drink. Down on the eighth level Daggies are hard at work drilling. How far they drill is beyond me.

"On the Earthies rain? In the human world, it falls from the skies by the barrelful. End of subject.

"Don't you get any ideas about sinking to the eighth level? Hear me?"

"Who said anything about ideas, Hitty? Will you go with me to watch the Special Forces roll in to the security building?"

"They're due at 8:30 pm. We could stroll to the scene as if we're going to work. We can't stay long. I have to prepare for a midnight meeting with the mentoring crew."

"Mentoring crew? What's that?" Brat asked.

"You don't think I'm a free agent, do you? Mentors give account of themselves to their uppers."

"Account yourself ably, Hitty. Like the twins said, I wouldn't do well without you."

"I'll do it, Brat. Caution is on overdrive."

They ate and then walked toward the security building. The area was teeming with booted Daggies in black uniforms and black berets that topped their shorn heads. Occupants were being ejected from the apartment next to the security headquarters to house the special services.

"We had better run without a moment's delay, Brat. They're already here, and in cahoots with the local forces."

Brat was ten paces ahead as they raced to the safety of Hitty's unit.

"I'll scoot on home, Hitty. Save me a piece of brown bread," he said through his snorts and puffs.

Think I'll make a visit to Sadie for an official comment on our honored guests, Hitty thought on Brat's departure.

She bagged two Jasmine teas and went the back way to Sadie's building. *Hope she's home, and not in the hands of the revered forces.* Hitty gave a few taps on the door of unit 19. A tense whisper came in response, "Who is it?"

"Hitty. Let me in."

The door opened by inches and Hitty edged in.

"This is no time for you to be visiting me. What are you about?"

"Where else can I go to diffuse my dreary wondering? What are you doing home at this hour?"

"The Forces didn't throw us to the wolves like they did the inhabitants of building 20. They sent us home for a day until the question of room assignments is settled."

"Have the Monitors arrived yet?"

"Don't think so, or we would have been evacuated. That's the cheerful word the Forces are using."

"You can double with me if you get thrown...I mean evacuated."

"Your offer is accepted... I'll be at your door, Hitty."

"A tea to comfort you," Hitty said, putting the bag into Sadie's hand.

Hitty sat at the table a moment and then said, "Vexy is posted to the Internal Security section. Has she taken up residence yet?"

"She was in last night, flaunting her slinky self and blathering that she had an in with a big boss. If the big boss gets wind of her prating, she'll be sliding downstairs. The leaders of the security section are fearful of the dreaded word favoritism. No favors here except for the Head Honcho."

"A toxic instrument like Vexy finds a target. Mind your steps," Hitty said.

"Instrumental music in the copper mines is more her style," Sadie said. "My steps are in sync with her tuning fork."

Images of Vexy flitted through Hitty's mind. *Sadie may be shrewd,* she thought, *but Vexy is a clever Daggie.* She stopped off to buy the ingredients for soup on her way home. "Extra special meal?" the grocer asked with a raised eyebrow.

"A celebration of my twenty fifth year as a Mentor, Arl," Hitty said.

I had better mind my own steps and vary my grocers, she thought on her way home. *No time to fix lunch. Brat will have to wait for dinner.* She dressed and went to her review meeting with the director and staff of the mentoring program.

Brat ate lunch alone and studied half the night on the customs and habits of the humans. He waffled in his decision to stay at home for the week. *No use to take chances with these forces everywhere. Why berate the luckless humans if I haven't learned from them?* He decided to forego visiting Hitty to spend the time in study.

Tired from his studies he went to bed early. Still, he lay awake for an hour thinking about his earlier view of the security forces.

The images came when he was deep in slumber. He stood on a stage with a group of students dressed in light green and ivory, clothing. He looked into a sea of faces sitting in rows below him.

The same teacher as in his former dreams said, "Your fellow students are waiting for your report, Brad." The scene vanished and he slept undisturbed until nightfall.

Riddles and Forces are the bane of my life, he said to himself on arising. *At least I slept well. The dream is beginning to have a soothing effect.* He brewed tea and after showering he dressed and reviewed his class notes.

His door opened in the middle of the task and the twins walked in. "Sit right there," Luna said while she picked up two cups from the kitchen counter and poured tea into them. "A ginger loaf for you, too."

"Your skills in baking may get you a transfer to the culinary institute," Brat remarked as he was on his second sample of the loaf."

"Don't you dare mention such a thing," Luna said. "Baking is our secret."

"My lips are sealed. Let it remain in the trove of the undisclosed."

In class, they firmed up their visit to Vexy's office. The twins reported on their office observations and Brat read his case notes on human customs and conduct.

"Any plans for a stakeout on the humans?" Hassel asked.

"A visit to the lower orders might edify our dull routine," Brat said. "The upper ranks have been duly observed. Upper and lower? Do the terms mean the same here? "

"No. No upper ranks here. Equality is guaranteed to all. Even the staclets are equal in the nation of Dluse, except for HH's gigantic billets scattered over our planet."

"Perhaps the whole Netherworld?" Brat added.

"More or less," Hassel said and laughed. "Keep me informed on your plans to visit the billets of the humans."

On exiting the building, Brat noticed a vehicle moving along the street at a slow speed. "The forces are in high gear. Students may be exempt from their conniving, but inside is where safety lies. Scuttling on our feet will get us there," he said to the twins.

He left the twins at their doorway and took the alleyway to Hitty's.

"Chow is overdue, Hitty," he said as he flung the door open and marched in.

"Manners, Brat, manners. Can't you put your studies into practice?"

"Are you trying to get me arrested, Hitty?"

"Forget it. Sit and eat." She ladled soup into a bowl and set it before him. "My meetings went so well the wine store seduced me." She poured two small glasses of red wine from the bottle.

Brat raised his glass and said, "You outdid yourself. What meetings?"

"We Mentors passed the review easily. Then we held our monthly meeting of the Ward Mentors. We keep tabs on each other, share our pupil's progress, and keep up to date on graduate students.

"Students aren't in plentiful supply in this corner of the empire. Most of them tend to be indifferent pupils. The chosen ones, if there is any, go to the Head Honcho's territory on intake. The others are dispersed from here to there."

"I was a reject, chucked into your eager grasp, eh?"

"Who knows how you got here. How you escaped the Head Honcho's eye is beyond me. Vexy pinched the twins the year before you came. I exerted license and nabbed you from Unis."

"License? What's that?"

"As the president of our Ward Mentors, I can sometimes choose my student. My previous pupil had graduated and assumed her position in the Roads Department."

"If poor specimens are here, I wonder who the chosen and the in-between are."

"Revoke your wondering. Disaster lurks on that primrose path."

"In case it overtakes me, another bowl of soup will dull the pains of my ruin."

Hitty filled his bowl and said, "Prudence guides the steps of the wary."

"Your reminders are welcome as I take my leave and go into the darkness. Could you spare a bowl of soup or two to fortify me for the week? I'm staying indoors to study."

Hitty poured the rest of the soup into a container and said, "There goes my no sharing rule."

Brat paused at the door and said, "Remember the story you told me about the two giant beings snatching up the little ones?"

"Of course. Any swag is to be shared. Are you sharing?"

"None to share, Hitty. I'm sniffing for the trail, but I get lost in the thickets of confusion. "

"Sleep on it, Brat. Your dreams will bring an answer. Wait for it."

The Revolving Wheels

12

On the night of their visit to Vexy, Brat, and the twins, met with Hassel in the classroom.

"If pity existed here, my knee bows would get a workout before you, Hassel," Brat said.

Hassel laughed and said, "I'd be the first on my knees, Brat. Tact will get us a quick dismissal from Vexy. The office staff may not be overjoyed to see students who are outsiders to their ministrations."

Beterbe came to the doorway, brought his hands together in a silent gesture of goodwill, and vanished.

"Don't see Beterbe very often these nights," Hassel remarked.

Brat looked at him. "Solitary leanings? His recent absence from the office encouraged it, I expect."

The twins turned quizzical eyes on him, but at his hand signal, they remained quiet.

Hassel, watching their by-play, said nothing. He steered them into the street and began the parade to the security building.

They walked close to each other in a tense silence. The Forces forbade anyone to be outside except the workers going to or coming from work. Security officers filled the streets. Numerous vehicles were patrolling the various areas of town.

One vehicle approached as they neared the security building. Hassel showed his teacher ID and they were let go with a wave of the hand.

Built on the beehive model, the building, as all government structures, had an imposing entrance and interior atrium. The three-story building with wide terraced steps led up from the street with busts of HH on stately pillars. The office of Internal Security was on the second floor.

Vexy, waiting at the top of the stairs, escorted them into her workplace. There were ten desks in the room with nine faces raised to inspect them as they entered. One of the faces was Prye.

Vexy introduced them, "My brilliant students from my last position and their present teacher, Hassel. A tour of the office was granted to calm their distress when they learned I was leaving them."

Brat noted an eye roll at a back desk, and then the observant eyes looking him over with interest. She didn't speak during the following ten minutes, but continued her steady observation of him.

The occupants quickly stated their role in the unit. Prye mumbled his with a lowered head. Vexy detected restive movements among the staff, and at a signal fromthe personin back she ended her speech. "Busy, busy," she said and led them to the stairs.

"I'm pleased that you made this trip, Hassel. A view of my important position adds to the students morale. Sadie, the head of the unit, is my special friend."

"Which one is she?" Brat asked.

"Sitting in the back desk, the one who didn't speak. I have to emulate her quietness," Vexy tittered.

"Your sparkling personality demands an audience, quietness doesn't become you." Hassel smiled then said, "Surely she appreciates you as you are?"

"She has welcomed me graciously.

"Since I'm now in the security section our future contacts will be limited. We have to move on," she said, and expelled a long sigh. "Goodbye, lovelies." She blew a kiss to them as she stepped back into the office.

"There. Over and done," Hassel said as they stepped into the street. The roar of the security vehicles blended with the crimson glow in the background. A vehicle shadowed them to the educational building, which curbed any wish to speak.

In the safety of the classroom, Hassel said, "One question, and then the night is yours.

"How can you fit this field trip into your lesson plans?"

"Office layouts for us," Luna said. "We studied layouts the past week. Vexy's office seemed very crowded. Wim and I will have just five staff members."

"The five member office will be temporary, Luna. Beginners get a break. Within a year a larger office staff will be assigned to you," Hassel replied. "Your expertise will be on the line, so don't trip up."

"We won't, Hassel," Wim said. "We aim to be sticklers in our work."

"And you, Brat? What have you to say?"

"The inner workings of security remain obscure, but the view of their play-pen is useful. Gave me an idea of what's in store for us."

"I wouldn't use the term play-pen outside of class, Brat," Hassel cautioned. "The Indulgence of students only goes so far."

"Discretion is the word, Hassel. Sorry about that."

Brat dropped the twins off at their staclet, and said he planned to stay indoors for the week. "I'll be engrossed with the captivating company of the humans .I suggest an indoor study week for you also."

"You mean we ought to avoid the security services?"

"Correct. The Monitors will be here any night. Once they arrive, I suspect the Big Boss is right behind them.

Best to think ahead."

The week disappeared under the demands of study. When Brat surfaced he had a clear understanding of how humans sorted themselves into ethnic groups and classes.

Hitty was on his mind, and he took the back way to her staclet.

He opened the door and looked in. She was at the kitchen sink washing dishes. He spoke and she jumped a foot. "Brat! You startled me."

"What's happened to make you so jumpy?"

"The Monitors arrived tonight. That's why I'm so jittery."

"What is the role of the Monitors, Hitty?"

"Observation of the residents through closed circuit screens. I don't know the specifics, but you evaded their net by an hour. They haven't set up their equipment yet."

"Escaped their beady eyes by an hour, huh? The day on your settee will prevent trouble. Do you mind?"

"Safety first. Can you sleep on the settee?"

"I can. Where's the eats? A starving Daggie is in front of you."

"At your bidding, Brat. I'm a foolish Mentor to let your brashness override HH's rules. Set the table. If you have any energy to spare make us a cup of cappuccino for dessert."

"To the eats then while the coffee is perking. I've been thinking. Aside from eggs, our food is mainly veggies. From my reading, humans eat animals, fish, and birds. None of those creatures lives here. Have you any ideas on the subject?"

"You never let loose of the questions, Brat. I'm not a set of encyclopedias. I imagine it's because we live in cities. No animals of any kind live on our planet. No forests or water creatures are here either. Maybe they have more sense than to live here."

"Details are missing in your answer, but this stew is pleasing to my appetite. Better than the McDonald's hamburger I ate recently."

"McDonald's hamburger?"

"Tell you another time. Toss me a blanket and I'll catch some shut eye."

"A bit early for bed."

"Rest is required if I am to haunt a pleb who is unaware of my presence."

"I'll leave that one alone." Hitty took a blanket off her bed, tossed it to him, and then busied herself in washing the dishes.

A loud knock on the door roused them from slumber in late night. Through her tiny window, Hitty saw Sadie standing outside in her night clothes. She went to the door and brought her in.

"I'm thrown into the street," she said and folded her hands together in a plea.

"I've been expecting you. Come, meet another waif."

Brat, sat up on the settee and stared at Sadie with goggle eyes, and then said to Hitty, "I'm the one with the secrets, am I?"

She ignored his question and said, "Meet Sadie, Brat."

"Already met her," he said. "The class tour last week."

"Hello, Brat," Sadie said. "I didn't know Hitty boarded her trainees."

"Best to stay inside while the Monitors do their thing." Hitty replied. "And that includes Brat. We'll make do. In the drawer next to the bed is a dress that will fit you. Might as well have breakfast."

Brat put the coffee on and set the table while Sadie showered and changed. Hitty whispered, "Avoid talking while she's here." She filled the plates with scrambled eggs while Brat placed the spoons and forks on the table.

Sadie sat down at the table and said, "You don't have to use your pence for my visit, Hitty. A sumptuous meal like this is pricey."

"Don't fret, Sadie. How often do we have a meal together?"

"I'm in your debt again."

Brat sat quietly while Hitty and Sadie discussed security matters. He ate quickly, took his shower, dressed, and began to clear the table.

"Useful in the kitchen too, Hitty? Any chance you could lend him to me?"

"Not a chance, Sadie. He's slated to be the Director of the Intake Department. He's proving to be an obedient servant."

Brat, at the sink washing the dishes, turned his back to them and rolled his eyes.

Hitty showered and was in the process of dressing when the loudspeakers began blaring outside. "All Daggies assemble in the street to pay homage to our Sovereign Leader."

"Timing is perfect, Hitty," Sadie said. "The Monitors will vacate my apartment, load their equipment, and be gone by daylight.

"Brat, our acquaintance is cut short. Hitty tells me you're an unusual trainee, clever and talented. You don't talk much, do you?"

"A fool is known by his words, Sadie," Brat replied.

Hitty interrupted, "To the streets we go." They followed her into the street where Daggies were already congregating. Office and factory workers were coming from all directions. They stood densely packed behind the roped-off streets and conversed in low tones.

"I have to run home and get dressed in my uniform," Sadie said. "All the security ranks are posted in the streets to maintain order among the prols. If you would like, I can get you a spot in front."

"We would like," Hitty replied. A close-up of our great Leader? What an honor."

"Wait here until I return," Sadie said.

She was back in ten minutes, and the crowd had grown denser. Sadie pushed through the throng with Hitty and Brat in tow. She stationed them in the front ranks of the Daggies, and then went to join her security unit.

Brat expelled his breath in a muted sigh. "Longest I've been quiet. The stored words are likely to ignite."

"Don't ignite here. You'll be taken to the furnace as kindle for the coal."

"Look!" he murmured, and gestured toward Vexy who was walking into the street. She swung her truncheon, and ordered the Daggies standing behind the ropes to move farther back.

"A craven in her proper element," Hitty muttered through pursed lips.

"She's in her form-fitting uniform and knee high boots. She doesn't want to be missed," Brat said.

"Pushy Daggies aim for a fall," Hitty remarked.

A booming voice came from the loudspeakers positioned on top of the nearby buildings.

"Silence, Daggies. Our great Leader is approaching."

Through the pin-drop stillness came a deafening roar, and Brat felt a warm breeze waft over his face. A scarlet limousine with top down came into view and slowed as it approached the crowded streets. A line of black cars followed.

The security forces stepped behind the ropes and the scarlet vehicle proceeded. As it passed, Brat saw a huge figure sitting in the backseat. A black tunic covered his lower form completely. His dark hair, sleek and lustrous, fit close to his head. He sat erect and his handsome, but grim and forbidding, countenance turned towards the crowd.

His eyes passed over Vexy who was inching closer to the car, and for a moment Brat thought his gaze lingered on himself and Hitty.

The car moved past, and then sped away into the darkness. The loudspeakers dissolved the stillness. "Get back to work, Daggies. Devotion to your revered Leader will be shown by an extra hour of work tonight."

Hitty and Brat dispersed along with the other Daggies.

"This pageant has to be absorbed before we speak of it, Hitty. I must run home and cram in an extra hour of study to show my deference. Maybe you can bake a chocolate cake for your hour."

"All of a sudden, you're deferential, Brat. It's at the top of your list to cultivate? If so, include me in your deference."

"Gotta go, Hitty. Don't forget the chocolate cake." On his way, home Brat stopped off at the twins. Luna was at their tiny stove stirring a pot and Wim was setting the table.

"Come in, Brat, and relieve my anxiety," he said. "Luna is doing a broth to quell hers."

"We saw you and Hitty, but we couldn't get through the crowd to join you," Luna said. "Did you see the dreadful face of our Leader?"

"A face not to be trifled with," Brat replied. "He's busy at the capital in a distant country. Why would he be interested in rejects, like us? "

"Our trust frayed after Vexy's trick. He made us nervous, Brat. He looked so horrid."

"Tend the broth in tribute to his passing through, Luna. Hitty said his last visit was soon after her arrival, and that's been eons."

Two hours later, the twins were calm, and Brat went home to his studies. *No junkets tonight,* he said to himself. He sat at his desk with a map in front of him. He pored over it for an hour without forming a fixed plan for his assignment. *To the wilds of the Earthies I must go, but where?*

He laid the map aside and paged through a volume on The Everyday Life of the Ordinary Human. *I'll get Hitty's and Hassel's take on which group to choose.* He laid the book aside and reached for another in his small bookcase.

For the remainder of the night he focused on the Intake Department. From the statistical charts in the book, it was evident that most of the incoming residents were Earthlings. *Hopeless humans. They are a lively bunch. Think I'm growing fond of them.*

He went to bed at dawn, and the Leader's face, fierce and merciless, loomed over him throughout his day's sleep. Tired and restless from his broken sleep, he arose before nightfall. *Wish the dreams would get lost. Enough already!*

When Brat had showered and dressed, he took his class notes and went by way of the twins. They were sitting outside on the steps of their building. "Waiting for you, Brat," Luna said as he approached.

The streets were dark, and the soundless steps of the few workers going to, or coming from their shift added to the dismal scene. The Synlan staff had packed up and left the night before along with the Security Forces.

Hassel greeted them with a hand wave and a cheery hello when they entered the classroom.

"Are you promoting cheer for Swinne, Hassel?" Brat asked.

"Not so much for Swinne as for Beterbe, Brat. He is moving on to the Educational Bureau as a personal assistant to the Director."

"He will be Swinne's superior?"

"He will be in the lofty circles that Swinne must bow to every five years. He will come in shortly to wish you and the twins goodbye."

The twins reported on their studies and discussed office internships with Hassel. They requested a placement in one of the Intake offices. "We want to be in Brat's department when he becomes Director of the Intake and Research Department," Wim said.

"I'll see what I can do for you," Hassel said.

Brat related the details of his study of the humans and said, "I want your input on the type of setting to choose for my last observation."

"We decided on someone from the labor category. You mean the region where they live, Brat?"

"That's it Hassel."

"I advise you to study the geography of the human world. Maybe, you would like to visit a mountain region. The setting is different from the urban ones you've visited."

"I'll check out the mountain regions tonight," Brat replied."

Beterbe came in and interrupted them, "I must be at my new posting next night. I will miss you everyone."

"We wish you well with your post, Beterbe," Brat said.

"I won't forget you, Brat. You are the rare student who has the respect of everyone in this department."

"Your recent performance is commendable, and a promotion is in your future, Wim and Luna."

He then went to his office, and Hassel dismissed the class.

The Hills Beckon

13

As Brat and the twins walked from the classroom, Beterbe signaled to Brat from the door of his office. He mouthed, "See you later."

"What did he want?" Luna asked him.

"To say he would miss us."

"At least one person who is high-up likes us," Wim said.

"We need all the help we can get in this place." Brat replied.

Once home, Brat changed into his overalls and hat, took a bag of the coins from the cranny, and made his way through the back way to Kruknsak's unit. He knocked on the door, and a quaver, "Who is it?" came from inside.

"Brat," he hissed.

The door opened, and Kruknsak ushered him in. "No time to waste Brat. I'm on my way to work."

Brat quickly told him about his son and handed him the bag of coins. "Be cautious in their use, may be the last I can bring you."

"You have brought me news that is worth more than all the coins in this land. I'll prize them as a gift from you and my son."

On leaving Kruknsak, Brat joined the wordless Daggies on their way to The Works. He soon dropped behind and made his way to Hitty's.

"Bring on the goodies I haven't had a decent meal since we ate with Sadie," he said as he threw the door open without knocking and strode to the kitchen table.

"Leaving my door open when you come in is flouting the Daggie custom of keeping everything shut."

"I'm practicing my loutish techniques. Where else can I practice if not on you?"

Hitty set her book on humans aside, and said, "I'm the coach, not you. You are to be a model Daggie with me, but loutish in other venue's. Save the louts for your director's job."

"I will amend my ways and flaunt your peerless coaching before Hassel and the twins."

"For the present, shut the door and we'll get on with my matchless coaching."

Brat shut the door, and Hitty went to the kitchen counter and filled two cups with tea. "I have to run for miles to buy our posh foods. All the Grocers in three Wards know me. We'd better be content with legumes and the regular tea for awhile."

"I'm with you, Hitty. We don't want attention. Did you see the Leader gazing from his hooded eyes at the Daggies when he passed by in that ruby red car of his?"

"And the hooded eyes lingered on you and me?"

"I wondered if you observed his gaze on us."

"Gave me chills, Hitty. That gaze hovered over me all day in my dreams. Where are the green clad creatures when we need them?"

"Green clad, Brat? No green around here. Shades of black and gray tinged with crimson fit us."

"I'm referring to my dreams of the green beings in the marble building."

"I'm afraid it's just you and me, not some dream beings."

"But you said to share the swag."

"Has there been any swag?"

"No. I'm sure to run up on it though."

"Until then, forget the green clad beings."

"Forgetting is not an option. However, another matter of the moment is pressing for a solution. My assignment is to observe a human from the laboring class. Your ideas are wanted since you have studied their habits."

"There's no lack of human workers. What's the problem?"

"Who to observe in a rural area? I pinpointed the region to visit in North America. It has hills and trees. I may get lost and you'll have to send out the rescue squad."

"No rescue squads here, Brat. Give me a copy of your route. As to the visit...why not choose a farmer? I expect choices are limited in a rural area."

They sat in a peaceful silence for a minute or two eating their food. Brat was mulling on whether to tell her about his visit to Kruknsak Jr..

"He rubbed his hand over his creased brow and said, "Trust is not a word used here, it may be forbidden for all I know. You are the trustworthy sort, so I want you to know I visited young Kruknsak again."

"No news to me that you did, Brat. I sort of expected you might."

"He gave me three more bags of coins and requested that his father be given one. Is there anything amiss with inviting you to my home?"

"Brat, you do like to breach the conventions. You tread on dangerous ground, and if you are exposed there will be no end of trouble."

"My invite, Hitty? I'm aware of the danger. If I'm snared in a trap, you mustn't be involved in anyway."

"No use bickering with you then." She put a finger to her lips, drew in a breath, and then exhaled. "Mentors frequently call on their trainees. Tomorrow night you will receive an official visit."

Brat stopped off at the library to map his route and look up the names of the humans in the area of his visit.

He made a copy and then went home to study the speech patterns of the hill people.

A farmer it will be in the hills. My books say level ground is best for farming. Must be more farms than one kind. He closed his eyes, put his finger on a name, looked at it, and said, *Here I come, Elisha Coots.*

A knock on the door interrupted his musings, and he opened the door to Beterbe.

"Came to say goodbye, Brat. Thanks aren't a word in our vocabulary, but I will offer it to you. I don't know how you did it when I was shifted back to my position. I won't ask you any questions. I'm certain you did the deed, however."

"A cup of tea, Beterbe? We'll not refer to any past happenings. Best to forget."

Brat made tea and set it on the table. They sat chatting about Beterbe's hopes for his new job.

"When I saw the opening at the EB I applied promptly. Anything to remove myself from Swinne's' sight. Since Vexy slipped from his clutches, he might target me again. If an occasion arises to be of help to you, Brat, I will return the favor."

After Beterbe left, Brat reviewed his map, strapped his light rucksack on, donned his tunic, and went by way of Hitty's. He shoved the copy of the map under her door and started on his journey.

Two hours later, Brat, caught in the leafy branch of a tree, freed himself with effort. He dropped to the ground, brushed off the twigs, and examined his surroundings. A log house stood against the brow of a hill in the distance.

The sun was yet above the horizon. Brat glanced at his watch and saw it was late afternoon. A small building caught his eye. He opened the door, crawled into a pile of corn, scooped out a place to lie down, and spread his tunic on the floor. *Forgot the time difference in this section of the country,* he thought with a wry grimace.

The low voice of a man penetrated his sleep, and he sat up abruptly. "Them durn furriners hev lef' a baby in my corn crib," the man said. "Git outta thar littlun." He reached through the door to pick Brat up.

Brat, panicky, scooted farther into the corn piles and said, "I'm not a littlun, I'm one of your adults."

White hair and a pepper and salt beard that fell to his chest framed the face staring at him. His denim shirt and overalls clothed a stocky body, and his eyes had a puzzled expression.

The farmer gazed at him for a moment and then said, "Ye air the pitcher of a baby. No grown man air two feet tall. Look at them yers of yourn."

"My yers, as you call them, are perfectly normal," Brat retorted indignantly. "I'm two feet and a half tall, thank you."

"Lemme see ye walk," the farmer said. "Cum outta thar."

Brat rolled off the corn, rummaged underneath a heap, and pulled his tunic free.

"If ye git outta the way, I won't hitcha when I jump outta the door," Brat said.

"Ye air a spry littlun. Ifen ye cum hyar ye can hep me feed the chickens, and we'uns can hev a bite of supper attur they eat."

We'uns can eat supper any time, I air hungry," Brat said as he hopped to the ground.

"Hol' on til the chickens git ther feed. I air cravin' eggs fer brekas."

"I like'em," Brat said. "Do them chickens like eggs too?"

He looked around at what appeared to be big birds running toward them. The birds were making funny noises, and some of them had tiny fluffy ones following them.

"Ye air a funny feller, but you air a littlun. Whut's that thang on yore back?"

"That thar thang is my backpack," Brat said. "Whut is the birds a doin?"

They ain't birds. They air chickens that lay the eggs I be eatin' fer brekas."

"Seems a shame they can't enjoy their own eggs," Brat said.

"You air a funny feller. Cum here and hull the corn wit' me. We can set on the log over thar." He handed Brat an ear of corn and showed him how to shuck it and shell the grains into a pan.

"Whut wuz ye doin' a sleepin' in my crib if ye ain't a baby?" the farmer asked.

"Beats me," Brat replied. "Tell me whut air them fluffy chickens." He pointed to the baby chicks.

"They air babies of the hens. They grow in the eggs."

"Doncha' tell me no more," Bat replied. "It's a gittin' sumwhut knotty."

"Ye air a baby." The farmer laughed, stood up, and said, "We done hulled enuff. Cum'on ye hens, and git hit."

He threw the corn in the direction of the chickens that were competing with each other to get to the grains of corn.

"Whut's the racket they air makin'?" Brat asked.

"They air clukin' and cacklin'. Ma useta' say the womenfok's clucked and cackled when they wuz quiltin' down at the church house. "

"Is Ma in the house?"

"Ma done passed on," the farmer said and pointed upwards to the sky.

Brat followed his gaze, and then remembered his reading on the life span of a human.

"Whut's yore name?" the farmer asked.

"I air Brat and yore name is Elisha."

Astonished, the farmer stared at Brat and said, "How didcha' larn my name?"

"You air known in these parts, that's how. Who air the furriners? "

"They'uns cum frum the city and set to farmin' ten yers back. A bunch of 'em live up the holler o'er Grady Branch way. They be purty pore." He put the pan in the corn crib and said, "We'uns air goin' in fer eatin. Don' fix much since Ma's gone. Ol' Betsy giz me milk an' thars buttermilk a plenny."

"Ol' Betsy? Who air her?" Brat asked.

"She air my cow, and a good'un she air too."

His study of agricultural life came to Brat's memory, and he said, "Whars ol' Betsy?"

"She be in the barn. I done milked her."

"I air cravin' to set my eyes on'er. We'uns can do the eatin' attur that."

"You air a funny feller. Ain't ye seen a cow a 'fore?"

"Not ol' Betsy. I wanna' thank her fer the milk."

"Cum' wit me, littlun. Ol' Betsy be sleepin' attur she et her supper."

They walked to the barn in the dimming light of evening. Brat looked inside the small log building and saw a huge beast lying on a mound of hay.

"Ol'Betsy be right smart high. Air she a ridin' critter?" Brat asked.

The farmer looked at him in surprise and said, "Cows don't be fer ridin,' hosses be fer ridin.' A baby ye air and ain't been to schoolin'. Them furriners ain't larned ye nothin'."

"I ain't no furriner," Brat retorted. "I air larnin' whar I live ever night."

"Littlun, ye cum stay wit me, and ye be larnin' in the day time. Ye wanna see them hogs o' mine a 'fore we eat?"

"Lead on, Elisha. I be right partial to the critters," Brat said.

"Call me Lish if you wanna. Ma and uttur folks allus do hit."

"Whars the hogs, Lish? Do they'uns hev babies?"

"Sukie air the mommy of one baby. She be feedin' it."

"They be a squealin', Lish. Whut air they'uns a sayin'?" Brat asked.

"She air a gruntin,' not talkin.' The baby's a squeal-in.' Hogs don' say no words."

Brat went to a fenced in pen and gazed through the slats at two pigs lying in a pile of hay. The baby pig glanced at him and then returned to its suckling.

"He air eatin' supper," Elisha said and chuckled.

"That air a fair way for a baby to git supper." Brat said.

"Don' look like ye be weaned vary long," Elisha said.

"Whut's the meanin' o' that, Lish?"

"The babies don' hev ther mommy's milk no more."

"I niver hed a mommy's milk. A glass is whut I be drankin' frum."

"A pore chile you air, Brat. Attur supper, weuns will lissen to the banjer.

Brat followed Elisha into the house where a fireplace crackled, and the flames danced merrily. A bucket on the hearth was filled with coal, and a wooden box nearby was piled high with wood. In one corner stood a shelf filled with books that looked well-read. Brat went near and read on the books spines: Plato, Gibbons, and Eusebius, among others. "You study too, Lish?"

"I be readin, Brat, since I was a littlun. My pappy said he never saw sich in all his born days, but he let me do my readin'."

Brat looked at the coal in the bucket and said, "You hev coal, Lish? Air ye diggin' in the ground fer hit?"

"Thar air miners o'er to Kinner Fork diggin' fer it. I hev a passel that wuz my pappy's and his pappy's a 'fore him. I ain't beholdin' to nary one.

"I fixed a kittle uv beans yestiddy. Thars cornbread and buttermilk, enuff for us," Elisha said as he washed and dried his hands.

"Warsh yore hands...hurr lemme hep ye. Stan' on thiz cherr." Elisha placed a chair by the wash stand, went into another room, and came back with a large cushion. He placed it in a chair at the table while Brat washed and dried his hands.

"Ye air kin,' Lish," he said and sprang into the chair.

"Ye air a spry littlun," Elisha said admiringly as he passed a bowl of beans to him. He placed the cornbread and milk on the table and sat down beside Brat.

"I got cookies fer us in my backpack, Lish, when we git through thiz here fine food. 'Most a fine as Hitty's."

"Whar didcha' git a cookie? Them furriners are pore. Look at ye. Them ain't ever carried ye to Dr. Maler. On'y three fangers on them teensy han's o' yourn'."

"I ain't a furriner, Lish. My fangers fit dish warshin' right well."

"Ye can rinch and dry the dishes fer me ifen ye stan' on yore cherr." Brat rinsed and dried the dishes while Elisha put them away.

Then Elisha took his banjo from the wall, and Brat fetched his cookies. They sat eating while Elisha played the tunes of the hills.

An hour later the farmer glanced at the clock on the wall and said, "Hit air time we'uns be in bed. Betsy git's outta the barn erly. I been readin' early church history. Time for a chapter or two a 'fore I sleep.

"Yore banjer pickin' wuz mighty good Lish. I niver heard music like that a 'fore. Wish we coulda talked about yore book larnin'"

"My pappy larned me banjo pickin, Brat. I wuz nigh a littlun as ye be. I larned the books myself."

He got up, hung his banjo on the wall, and opened a door to an extra bedroom. "Hyar's a place fer ye to sleep. If ye git col,' thar's extry kiver on the cherr. Hit gits purty nippy in the night."

"Goodnight, Lish. Ye be a man o' parts. Hit's a gladsome time we had tonight."

Brat lay on the bed until he heard the sound of snoring and knew that it was safe to leave. He penned a note and stuck it under the bedroom door. Next, he stowed his tunic in the rucksack, fastened it to his back, and went into the night.

When Brat sat down from his flight on a back street, he paused and thought about going to Hitty's. He looked at his watch, and then noted the approach of dawn by streamers of coral across the horizon. He went home and slept the day away. Dreams of Elisha and the animals filled the hours while the green clad beings sat on the sideline and watched. On awakening, he dressed and sped to Hitty's.

"I'm back and ready for brekas. Tussling with trees and leaves has left me famished." He handed her a bag. "One of these bagels might be jest right."

"Nothing to eat while you were in the hills, Brat?" Hitty said while taking out a pan and placing it on the hotplate. "You learned some new phrases from observing the humans?"

"I did both. Elisha fed me and showed me Sukie the pig and Betsy the cow. The adult chickens grow chicks and the eggs we eat. It must be the generating thing. We ate, and then he played his banjo.

"The food was satisfying, almost as good as yours. I'm laying off the bacon. Pigs like Sukey and her piglet are fated to be done in for our enjoyment."

"Brat, you are a wonder and likely to be fated for The Works if you linger on the kindly way. Benevolence doesn't live here. Malice has a lodging in every quarter of this town, and prowls nightly among the denizens.

"Now get busy and make the coffee. My more than satisfactory hot bagels are ripe for eating. We'll discuss this amazing trip of yours in more detail over our munching."

While Brat sat eating and sharing his tale from the hills with Hitty, an incident that affected his future had happened the night before.

Wheels within Wheels

14

Far off in the netherworld, in the city of Synlan, capital of Dluse, a multitude of workers sat at central processing machines on the twenty-fifth floor of a high-rise building. Their function was to monitor the human world and Daganland. An outpost, where the young and old were routinely sent, Daganland seldom received any monitoring. Their bureaucratic posts were filled by assignment from the capital, or by the young Daggies who came through their Intake Department.

One of the monitors, Sena, happened to scroll to Daganland and watched Brat descend on the back street.

"Hey, you guys, here's a Daggie that seems to be a member of the smart set."

Those sitting near her laughed and dismissed her remark.

But what she had seen intrigued her, and throughout the following weeks, she monitored Daganland. What she observed provided a fascinating glimpse into their politics and the life of a smart Daggie.

Brat's sleep was filled with the green clad beings walking the marble streets of a city. He felt the soft warmth of the sunshine and gazed at the patterns of light and shadow on the sidewalk. Then he was onstage again with the instructor. The auditorium was filled with students who were looking at him expectantly. "We're waiting to hear your story of Elisha, Brad," the instructor said.

On awakening, he sat for a while on the side of the bed and reviewed his dream of the radiant beings. *A world within a world, I'd like to exchange my night life for my day life.*

Later, when Brat and the twins entered the classroom, he noted Hassel's excitement.

After their reports were given, Hassel said, "For your info only. A snafu in Vexy's security unit led to a fellow worker telling her that he did private work in his off hours. She went to Sadie's superior flouting the rule of authority. Prye, who foolishly revealed his misdeeds, is fated for hard labor on the road detail while Vexy revels in her patriotic duty."

Brat sat silent, engrossed in thought, as Hassel spoke. On class dismissal he told the twins, "I'll be over later." He then went to Hitty's.

<hr />

"Have you heard about Vexy," he asked as he entered in a rush, and shut the door behind him.

'Calm down, Brat. Let's have tea and be rational on the subject of Vexy."

She motioned for him to sit at the table and said, "I've gotten the news from Sadie who is red-hot because her authority was ignored. A reprimand from her boss magnified her anger. Sadie's bad list has a new name. We'll wait for further developments in that quarter.

"Prye has undoubtedly revealed his dealings with you and me. Mentors are permitted certain liberties with their pupils, so I'm likely to escape a penalty. I'm in for a stern questioning, however. You may not be so lucky, but the sentence will be light, for your stellar record speaks for itself."

"How will my studies be affected?"

"Serving a sentence, no matter how long or short isn't a hindrance in the job line. No offense records are kept. Many associates of the Head Honcho came up from the lower floors."

"He must be hard up for associates."

"Says you and me. Fen, the director of his Security Services, was a former general in the armed services of a human country. HH recruited him from Akka, a town in the western district of Dluse, where he toiled in the furnace repair division. Most of the upper rank members in Fen's security force have similar records."

"Interesting tidbit to know, Hitty, but the near problem is Vexy who is a lethal weapon. She needs reigning in. Who's going to do it?"

"Sadie is a very clever manipulator," Hitty replied.

"She didn't get her position by being nice. She'll put the word out on Vexy, and before long; it will reach all the security branches. Give her a month or so."

"If I'm sentenced, will my studies be put on hold?" Brat asked.

"Of course not. You can continue your studies on the job. On return, you will pick up where you left off."

"Think I'll run away to the hills and stay with Lish."

"You can't make a run for it. No matter where you go the security forces will be right behind you. Why do you think the GPS is in the library? Each time you punch in your destination the info goes into the central office of the Big Boss's security forces."

Brat looked at her with a furrowed brow and indrawn breath. He expelled a long sigh, stood up, and said, "Tonight is the night for our dinner. Knock on my door in an hour, and bring a pot of soup. My input is desert."

Hitty showed within the hour bundled in her heaviest tunic and hunched over like one of the Daggies from the mining pits.

"If my Daggie sins mean a spell in the ovens, let me be well fed to meet my fate." Brat said on opening the door to her.

He was rather subdued during their meal. He brewed a pot of tea after dinner, and both sat glumly looking at their cups. "Hitty, do you believe in love?" he finally asked her.

"I have never thought on the term, Brat. It's in the Earthling dictionary, but the word slips by me without meaning."

"Remember the first family I visited with the young one? They loved one another. I didn't understand what it was at the time, but I do now. It's why I was uneasy with the boy's response to my pestering him.

"When I talked to Lish the meaning of the word love became clear. He didn't care if I looked different. For the hours I knew him, he treated me kindly and invited me to live with him. I was tempted, but I thought of you. Did you ever love anyone, Hitty?"

"When you ask me that question, Brat, you're the only one that comes to mind. I've read how the human mothers feel about their young. It describes the feeling I have for you, so I guess it is love."

"Well, here we are then. My dreams have focused on the green clad beings lately, and I rather identify with them. They seem to be in a place where love lives. Too bad we can't get there."

"Not likely, Brat. We had better tend to the matters in hand. Love doesn't live here, and dreams are best ignored."

"Any more thoughts on the white house you spoke to me about?"

"Memories, Brat? None yet. If any stop in, I'll info you."

Brat rose and went to his cache of coins, took out two bags, and placed them before Hitty. "Keep these until I get back."

Hitty went home with an emotion she had never felt before. *It's enough to make me want to wring my hands like Luna,* she said to herself.

When Hitty had gone, Brat dumped his costly items of food, save one. He bagged a chocolate sweet and went to see the twins.

Luna, with soggy tissue in hand, ran to the door when his knock came. "I'm so scared, Brat. Vexy is mean."

"Dry your tears and serve these goodies. Forget about Vexy. She's not likely to bother us sprats. I came to tell you that I might be away for a while. Don't worry; I'll be back when my affairs are settled."

"Oh, Brat, how will we manage without you? Affairs? What affairs?" Luna said, wringing her hands.

Wim said, "Don't fuss so much, Sis."

"Can you tell us where you're going, Brat?"

"Save the telling until I get home, Wim."

Brat sat chatting for an hour with them. He then went home to an uneasy sleep.

Sena was not the only one to have an interest in Brat. Someone else had him in mind. At the Synlan palace, the Head Honcho and his chief officers were closing an administrative meeting.

After the meeting broke, the Head Honcho leaned back in his chair and said to his security chief, "Fen, I noticed a Daggie youth when I passed through Nofer. I want him located and brought to me. And while you're at it, check out the female officer directing traffic near him. She was showing off, attracting attention."

Fen said, "Yes, Sir, right away."

"Get on it then," the Head Honcho said curtly. "Check with security. A female Daggie was standing with the youth. Get her name too."

In his office, Fen called Og and Viln and ordered them to get searching for Brat and Hitty and the female security officer. "Go easy," he said to them, "Four weeks should do it. The schedule of HH is so packed he spins his wheels both day and night. Daggies can't be that important."

Vexy was in a quandary. She knew that Brat and Hitty were implicated in Prye's crime, but she feared to disclose it after her scheme went awry with the twins and Hassel. Days of fretful sleep and jittery nerves only increased her fear. She went to work with bleary eyes, and when Sadie noticed her frazzled look, she asked the reason why.

Vexy then spoke to her of Hitty's and Brat's participation in Prye's after hours work.

Sadie listened to her with brows raised and lips indrawn.

"A mess you've made for us," she said. "Go to Delfie and tell her. You have no other recourse. Our whole unit is in jeopardy if it becomes known."

Vexy went upstairs and entered Delfie's office. In a stammering voice she related Prye's connection to Hitty and Brat. She came back with a mortified look on her face. Five minutes went by, and then with eyes downcast, she approached Sadie. "I have to arrest Brat. Delfie said his being a student doesn't matter."

"I'll see Delfie when the shift ends," Sadie said. "Wait until nightfall to arrest Brat."

Before dawn, Hitty was sitting with Sadie at her kitchen table. "Come to the office at 11 pm for your heartless session with Delfie. Wherever Vexy goes, it results in a disaster for someone. Her next disaster just might be hers. We have to make the best of this mess. Brat will have to serve a sentence of three months at The Works."

Brat's sleep was fitful throughout the day. He arose in early evening, *No use to wrestle against the fix I'm in. Better to work on my skills of survival. The buzz of caf-*

feine is called for. He brewed the coffee and was on his third cup when the expected knock on his door came.

Vexy said in a muffled voice, "It's me, Brat."

He opened the door and said, "Taking the night air, Vexy?"

"I've been sent to arrest you, Brat. Get your personal items and a change of clothes, the worst ones you own, and come with me."

"Why am I being arrested, Vexy?"

"Prye ratted on his clients, and you were one of them."

"I can't deny it. It's fitting that you arrest me. I'll be sent to The Works?"

"Yes, but I had nothing to do with it, Brat. It's the order of my boss. I wouldn't be so mean to you."

Brat strapped on his backpack, filled with a few belongings, and Vexy took him to the court of the magistrate. The building was a large two-story structure built of dark gray stone. It blended into the darkness and only the small windows reflected its existence. Large red eyes glared at them from the top of the pillars on each side of the wide steps leading upward to the front door. "They are busts of the Head Honcho," Vexy said.

Brat felt as if the eyes were following him as he and Vexy ascended the steps. Once inside they were directed to a room off the main entrance where a Daggie sat behind a desk staring at them with eyebrows drawn together. No one else was in the room except another Daggie who barked, "Step forward," at them.

Brat and Vexy stood in front of the Magistrate who looked sternly at Brat and said, "Young Daggie, you have been remiss in conduct. Three months on The Works detail.

"Take him down," he said banging his gavel loudly.

And Vexy did.

They walked in silence until the outer precincts of The Works came into view. Toiling silhouettes of the workers could be glimpsed against the flames leaping and dancing in the darkness. "Will you tell Hitty and Hassel where I am?"

"I'll tell them, Brat. Whatever did you do? I'm in the dumps with Sadie and now with Hitty. I wish she was going to The Works instead of you," she grumbled.

"No matter, I'll survive. I'm to blame, not Hitty. I was being a prankster."

"Pranksters don't fit into our customs. If not for your excellent record you would be serving a year's sentence."

"Maybe, I learn the hard way, Vexy. I'm learning though."

"We have to abide by the rules, Brat. Here we are at number 9 furnace works."

She took him into a building near the furnace and introduced him to a Mr. Faln.

"Do your work, Brat. I'll come for you in three months," Vexy said, and left him.

Brat gazed at the roaring furnace and the Daggies bustling back and forth with buckets full of coal to feed the insatiable fire. He drew in his breath and expelled a long sigh, "Where's my bucket. Might as well start," he said to Mr. Faln."

"Don't be so eager, young Daggie. Stow your things in your quarters and explore the layout of the furnace works."

Brat was taken to a large shelter with numerous beds in it. A storage locker was alongside each bed. He put his bag in his assigned locker and went out to survey his new surroundings.

Most of the coal bucket brigade were young and covered in black dust from head to foot. They stared at him through red eyes like little flames set in their soot-covered faces. *Not Swinne's beauty mask,* he thought as he stared in return.

"Let's make the coal hauling more efficient," he said to the youngster nearest him.

"I'm game. Tell us how and call me Jac."

"My name is Brat, Jac, and it's this way. We form a line and pass the buckets of coal along the line to the furnace."

"We could ask Mr. Faln to let us try it," Jac said.

Brat went to his quarters, changed into his grubby overalls, and approached Mr. Faln. "A bucket if you please and I'll get started."

"Never met an eager Daggie like you," Mr. Faln said, handing him a bucket. "The young get a break. Showers and six-hour shifts. You are on the first shift."

Brat said, "Do you mind if we try to make the coal hauling more efficient."

"Try away for three days. I've heard that you are clever."

And so, Brat began his career in the furnace Brigade.

Sena, in the meantime, watched Brat's plight with keen interest. Her fellow workers expressed no interest in Daganland, but she kept notes each night on Brat's activities. She also added Vexy to her list. She became so keen that she ran the film back a year and stayed late at the office to watch them.

She viewed Swinne and Vexy conspiring to send the twins to The Works. Then she ran an earlier film of Swinne raging at Beterbe for daring to imply that Vexy was out of control. She scrolled to the present films and studied Brat's visits to the humans. "That Daggie doesn't belong in Daganland," she said aloud to co-workers. "Wonder how he got there." Before long, someone else would be wondering too.

Three weeks went by, and Hitty and the twins developed a ritual of standing outside Brat's place of work to catch a glimpse of him. He hid his grief and obeyed the rule that banned contact with outsiders.

However, events were happening in other spheres to alter his predicament.

The Head Honcho inquired of Fen one night if he had located the young Daggie. "Not yet, we're working on it," Fen replied.

"That young Daggie better be in my office within a week," HH roared, "or I'll have your head."

Og and Viln had to work a double shift after calling the security monitors. It took them a night and a day to locate anyone in the unit with knowledge of Daganland. At last, Sena came forward with her notes and tapes. Two more nights went by while the tapes entertained the whole section. They gleefully watched as Brat was taken to The Works. In the last tape, he was an assistant to Mr. Faln.

"Aghast, the head of the section, Mr. Slack said, "If he comes here he'll have us on an efficiency schedule."

Og called for all the tapes on Daganland relating to the educational office, which took a night. Everyone rushed about the building while the manager Lax threw tantrums. A half dozen were found and sent to Fen.

Fen took the tapes and scrolled through them three times. Then he handed them over to the Head Honcho who viewed them while muttering invectives. He watched Brat's activities in the human world, his visit to Swinne, and his performance in the classroom.

When he viewed the tapes of Brat's visit to Husslm, and his novel tactics to obtain the coins and win the horse race, his dour face crinkled up and he emitted noises that resembled laughter. He viewed Vexy taking Brat to The Works and muttered some more invectives.

"The young fellow has possibilities. Get him for me, Fen. I'll make him my assistant. Never mind the female he was standing with as we drove by.

"The female Vexy was the one showing off when we drove through Nofer. She's to be moved to the fourth level and assigned to the group of philosophers spouting on Being and Nothingness. A six months sentence of listening to them will cure her of ambition and flouncing about."

He muttered under his breath, *and then she'll be ready for your position. Think, I don't know about your laziness.*

"While you're at it, send Swinne and Slack to the pig farm in Molek for re-education." *You will join them before too many moons have passed,* HH said to himself with a fiendish grin on his cruel face.

"The Daggies need to be restrained before we have trouble with them. Order your forces to monitor them more closely. Promote Sena to manage the security section while Slack is gone. The female loyalty is proving greater than the males."

"Yes Sir. Tonight Sir," Fen replied.

Fen went to his office, rubbing his hands together in delight, and bellowed, "Og, Viln, get in here. The boss is on a chase and the games begin."

Back in Daganland, Brat, hot, tired and sooty, went to work, ate and slept. When time allowed, he studied procedures for the Intake department. By the third week, his student life seemed to be receding into a distant past. He settled into the rhythm of the demanding job. In addition to his regular duties, he organized coal brigades at other furnaces under Faln's supervision

Each night as his shift ended, Hitty and the twins were waiting to see him. They were shadow dancers against the roaring flames as they waved and called to him.

Faln relented as the weeks passed and delivered their messages to Brat. By the end of the fourth week, the word came that Vexy had been arrested. Hitty next brought the news that Hassel had been chosen to head the department of education She was now the twins, Mentor. Swinne had been sent for re-education somewhere in a rural area.

All this drama and I'm not in it, Brat thought. *Enough to make me weep.*

Then, three nights later, Faln relayed the news that a security officer had come by earlier. "The Big Boss is looking for Brat," he said. "He's sending Fen to cart him to Synlan."

Faln relayed the news to Brat with uplifted eyebrows and said, "Best go to your quarters for the duration of the shift." Brat passed his bucket to Jac and nodded for him to take over.

He went to the shelter with an inner groan. *Oh my, what a pickle I've gotten myself in. HH is after me and the Gulag will be my home for ten years. Fight or flight?*

The Wheel Turns

15

Brat pondered his options for the next hour and then remembered his map of Synlan. *No use to fight. Hate to admit it, but HH is bigger than I am. Synlan is the safest bet.* He went to the door and checked for any passersby. *I Might need my blue uniform and scrip*, he thought. Seeing no one, he slipped out and made his way home by the back way.

His unit had been searched with all his belongings strewn about the room. His niche and his coins were intact, however. The map of Synlan lay on his desk untouched. He breathed a sigh of relief, put the uniform on, and stuffed his pockets full of coins. He fastened his tunic tightly, zipped up the front, nipped into the alley, and took his flight.

He arrived at his destination before sunrise. The streets were empty of pedestrians and an eerie silence seemed to flow from the cobbled streets. He scanned his surroundings, and saw a sign in big letters. 'Hotel Nero' was blinking in black and red letters. He went to the entrance and gazed at the inside lobby of red walls and black trimming. A huge photo of the Head Honcho stared at him from one of the walls. *Watching us, no doubt,* Brat said to himself.

Rows of tables with two chairs at each one were placed near the large front windows. *Not as luxurious as Vegas, but this will do.* He walked in and approached the desk occupied by an elderly clerk.

"Welcome to Synlan, young fellow. Are you here for the convention of the Security Forces?"

"Why else would I be here if not for the convention," Brat replied in a questioning tone.

"Right o' young fellow. Number 16 is vacant. To-night is the parade and Fen will be leading it. Is your brigade from...where are you from?"

"I'm from Lexter on the East coast," Brat replied, hoping fervently the clerk had never heard of Lexter. "And my brigade will be joining the others. Do you know Mr. Fen?"

"No. He's one of the bigwigs. He and HH are quite chummy. They have no time for the likes of me."

Brat took the key and busied himself with thoughts of Fen, but tired from his long flight he was soon snoozing in bed.

He awoke in the early evening, showered, and brushed his uniform before putting it on. *We Daggies have less luxuries than the Synlanese. No hotels, but the same architecture. The beehive mode moves on.*

An hour later, he peeked out the window and saw crowds massing on the sidewalks. "The parade," the clerk said. "Better get going or you'll be late."

"Guess I'd better at that," Brat replied. He stepped warily from the entrance and saw black uniforms filling the streets. Brown uniforms were visible, but very few blue ones were in the mix. He kept in the rear of the crowds and had reached the end of the line of black security forces when an officer spotted him and said, "Hey, you. What are you doing?"

"I'm joining my unit," Brat replied.

"Oh, you must be one of our fresh recruits."

"Hey, Rog," he said to a young chap. "Take him to the supply depot and see that he's dressed in our uniform,"

The chap stepped from the line and said, "Yes Sir, then he motioned for Brat to follow him.

In ten minutes, they stopped at a building and went in. "Rog here. A black uniform, if you please, for this little rogue."

Composed, Brat kept quiet and thought, *Little? You're only two inches taller than I am.*

Brat quickly donned the uniform including beret and boots. Rog said, "Hair cut later."

"Whose division are we in?" Brat asked as they jogged back to the line.

"Thought you knew. We're in Fen's outfit."

Brat quickly covered his gaffe by saying, "I mean company."

"We report directly to Fen and HH," Rog said. "An orientation session is scheduled tomorrow night for the new recruits. Do well on the entrance exam and you will earn a bigger unit in Building G. Incidentally what is your name?"

Brat groaned inwardly. *Ran towards the threat and here I am right in the nest of HH.* "Bo," he replied with a hollow feeling in his stomach.

Rog directed him to the back of the line, and Brat imitated the movements of the other members during the parade.

It was late night when the festivities were over and he returned to the hotel. *Hitty, Hitty, I need Hitty,* he thought morosely. An hour later, he said to himself, *I'm on my own. Might as well get on with it.* The dream of the green clad beings filled his hours of sleep. "You are not alone, Brat," one of them said. "Remember Lydo."

An undoubted wish fulfillment, he thought as he finished dressing and went to eat breakfast. The clerk at the desk handed him a notice. He was to report for orientation within the hour.

Two dozen recruits were in the room when Brat entered. He was given a file and ordered to take a seat in the front row. He gazed around the room and noticed an officer sitting against the wall near the door. He had a curl to his lips, and his hard eyes were roving over the recruits in the room. Another officer stood at the front of the group and welcomed them to Synlan, "You are the elect few who are chosen to serve our great Leader." He then directed them to open the file and take a test.

Brat looked at the test of mathematical symbols and astronomical calculations. Somehow, they reminded him of his dream chart, and he soon finished the test. *What stars do HH and Fen wander under?* He said to himself while looking at the officer sitting against the back wall.

They were dismissed without further instructions when the testing hour ended. The recruits filed from the room silently and entered the street without speaking. Brat returned to the hotel and asked the desk clerk for directions to the library.

See this play to the end or else what? Since I don't have a what, guess it'll be the play, he thought while walking the ten blocks to the library. He asked for books on astronomy and passed the hours away in the study of the different universes.

He was drawn to one particular galaxy far from Dluse. The galaxy Ourano was to his right at the top of the illustrated chart. The planet Lydo shone brightly. *Wish I was there,* he murmured wistfully.

The morning star was high on the horizon when he emerged from the library and trudged back to the hotel. "Where have you been," the desk clerk said waving his hands frantically. "The bigwig Fen is requesting your presence."

Brat's heart sank to his feet, and he remained rooted to the floor as wild thoughts passed through his mind.

Guess they found me out, he thought as he regained his composure. *Might as well face it.*

"Where am I to report?" He asked.

The clerk handed him a memo with a name and address on it. Fen, Head of Security, 113 Main Street, The Security Bureau. With a growing feeling of doom, Brat slowly walked the two blocks to the Bureau.

He took deep breaths at intervals to steady his nerves and paused to gaze at the structure in front of him. It was a replica of the government buildings in Daganland. *One size fits all,* Brat thought as he ascended the steps with the Head Honcho's red eyes following him.

He asked for Fen at the reception desk. A female took the memo from him and looked at it. "First time for this." she said widening her eyes in surprise. "I'll ring him." She pressed a button, then rose and escorted him to an office on the first floor.

Brat followed meekly and sat quietly in the waiting area until a door opened and a voice said, "Come in."

Back in Daganland, Fen's security officers went to The Works to apprehend Brat. After a fruitless search, Faln had a lot of explaining to do. And his garbled words couldn't be deciphered.

In Synlan, the Head Honcho raged at Fen and his assistants. Daganland got the brunt of Fen's anger. Faln and his young workers were grilled mercilessly, not excepting Hitty and the twins.

When the night passed without any progress in finding Brat, the Head Honcho began to suspect underhanded dealings. "I'm outwitted again, Fen. It happens every time." He scowled, and then sneered, "Those spies are trying my nerves. If they keep on, it's war."

Fen turned pale and stuttered, "Is t-that a go-od ide-a, HH?"

The Head Honcho turned on him and snarled, "Don't you dare mention the word good to me. You know that word isn't used here. You'll find yourself exiled to Daganland if you keep on."

Fen grew paler, threw his hands up in the air, and said, "No, no. Not Daganland."

"Mind what you say then. That young Daggie has outwitted you, and you'd better find him or...."

Back on Lydo, a monitor at a switching station watched the drama taking place at the capital of Dluse. Contact was immediate with the Academy. The director, Avrel, informed Professor Mikol who tuned in to the events happening in Brat's world.

"Let's see how he handles this turn of affairs," he said to Avrel. "We'll keep a close eye on him for a few days. HH cannot be allowed to pester him too much."

"That's the rub," Avrel said. "What is too much?"

"We'll know it when we see it," Professor Mikol said. "Brad may have put on a strange outer form, but his character hasn't. He has shown courage and ingenuity to an unusual degree. Just the traits we need in a future commander of our Supreme Lord's intergalactic forces."

Hitty and the twins had recovered from the grueling sessions with the security agents. However, their anxiety related to Brat's disappearance kept them on edge constantly. Vexy's arrest took backstage. They called on Hassel and Beterbe the only ones they dared approach. Neither one could offer any help. Thus, they remained in suspense and kept hoping that Brat would appear.

A new teacher arrived, Ms. Totech, and the twins attended to their studies under her instruction. They went to Hitty's after class and sat with her while she made dinner for the three of them.

On the second night, Hitty wrung her hands and said, "Something terrible must have happened. He may be in the Gulag."

Luna began to wring her hands and cry. Hitty calmed herself and said, "A cup of tea will do for us. Brat is probably on his way home. He's one tough Daggie."

The one tough Daggie entered the presence of Fen quivering inside. *Keep cool, Brat. Keep cool,* he said to himself as he approached Fen's desk and sat in the chair opposite him.

Fen stared at him with narrowed eyes, ran his finger over his lips, and said, "You're not much to look at. Your score on the test puzzles me. No one has ever gotten perfect marks before. You will go into my inner office and take another test." He pointed to a small room where an officer sat observing Brat.

Brat breathed a sigh of relief and took the file given him. He finished the longer and more difficult calculations in thirty minutes. The thought came to mind that perhaps the Gulag was rather to be preferred to this turn of events with Fen.

The officer picked up a book that had the test solutions and matched Brat's answers to them. All were correct.

"You came from Lexter? You must have superior schools," Fen said. "You will be my assistant and remain in this office." *If HH can have an assistant, so can I,* he mumbled to himself.

"Luc, take him to building G and see that he has an apartment. Then take him to the astronomy lab and introduce him to Commander Per."

Brat, rather numb from the proceedings went with the officer Luc to building G. The designs were similar to Daganland's, but Brat was given a larger unit with two rooms. "You can eat in the officers mess at headquarters," Luc said. "You will be in the office every night for six hours. Fen will dictate the duties to you."

Dictate is what I'm worried about, Brat thought.

Luc took him to the laboratory and introduced him to Commander Per who was in charge of intergalactic travel.

Brat stared at the strange being in front of him with frizzled gray hair framing his face and odd mannerisms. His sentences began and ended by eh.

"Eh, welcome young fellow, eh. Eh, come to learn, eh."

"My name is Bo, and it is an honor to study under your direction. I intend to learn the mapping of the routes we travel."

"Eh, glad to teach you, young fellow, eh," the Commander said.

The dawning light showed in the east as they exited the building. Luc sent Brat home to sleep and told him to come to Fen's office at twilight.

The black hole I'm in gets deeper and deeper, Brat thought as he walked to the hotel to inform the desk clerk that he was vacating his room. "Found a new berth, Bo?"

"I'll be at the G building," he replied.

"My advice is to watch your step, young fellow."

"I'm watching," Brat said. *Much good it's doing me,* he muttered under his breath. He ate in the snack bar and then went to his new home to sleep.

At dusk, he arose and discovered a shower in the second room made of glass. *Shades of Las Vegas,* he said to himself and reveled in the warmth of the water for an extra ten minutes. He dressed and decided to check in at the officers mess.

Security agents crowded the room, and Rog invited Brat to sit at his table.

"Hear you've snared a plum job," Rog said.

"News gets around fast in this burg," Bat replied. He noted the eyes on him from every part of the room.

"In your case, it did," Rog said. "The usual routine is for the rookies to get the scuff work. A lot of jealousy in the lower and upper ranks."

"I didn't seek the position. It sought me. Whatever your hands find to do...I don't know where that came from, but I will work and learn,"

His breakfast over, he went to Fen's office and asked Luc to explain his duties. "Keen to learn, are you, Bo? To begin, read these files. You will work here six hours each night and another two hours in the science lab."

Brat opened the first file and was stunned to find detailed documents of an espionage network focused on the planet Lydo. When he had read the last file, he suspected that his role was to devise means to thwart the Lydo monitors.

I have to let Hitty and the twins know where I am. How? Beterbe came to mind, but he dismissed the thought. He returned the files to Luc and said, "Can't wait to dive into action, Luc."

"Action it will be, Bo, within the year. Fen is relying on you to meet the goals of the Big Boss. My aid is yours if needed."

"Your aid is needed in one matter. I haven't had time to inform the Lexter security personnel of my promotion."

"How did you learn the physics and astronomy, Bo?" Luc asked.

"From my former life as a Homo sapien. Guess I was so dazed when I arrived the master of exams forgot to quiz me."

"A common problem for new arrivals. About your contact with security personnel? You will have a half night off next week. You can take care of the problem then."

Brat ate lunch in a cafe next door to avoid Rog, and then went to the astronomy lab. Commander Per laid a file filled with calculations on the table and a book on traveling cosmic routes. "Eh, it's your task to work on finding routes to Lydo that can't be easily tracked. No one has found even one so far, eh."

For the next week, Brat studied, slept, and read files on Lydo. At the lab, he began his calculations on loops and waves for interplanetary travel. His tasks were easy problems to solve, and an idea grew in his mind that he couldn't shake off.

At the end of the week, Brat went to see Hitty and the twins with a hope that no one was tracking him.

He checked his unit which was still vacant, dressed in his ordinary clothes, retrieved the few coins in the niche, and knocked on Hitty's door soon after.

Her eyes widened in disbelief at his entrance. She grabbed him, shook him back and forth, and said, "Where have you been? The twins and I have been frantic, fearing the worst had happened."

"I don't have time to explain. I'm in Synlan and assistant to Fen. I work at the science laboratory tracing astral pathways to the planet Lydo. Do you trust me Hitty?"

"I do, Brat. Why ask me that?"

"In two weeks I will come for you and the twins. Be ready and waiting. When you hear my knock, come out, and go to the back of the building. I dare not tell you more for your own safety."

Brat reclaimed his uniform and reached G building at midnight.

After her promotion, Sena no longer monitored the Daganland inhabitants. The other monitors had no interest in Nofer and neglected to tape any of the inhabitant's actions.

Fen's troubles were growing. He winced every time HH inquired if he had found the young Daggie. The mystery deepened, and his agents searched the country from one end to the other without results. The Nofer agents eventually put their search aside, and stopped at the pub every night.

Fen feared the wrath of HH and kept quiet about his new assistant. He knew that someone would reveal his secret any night, but in the meantime, he exulted in thinking he had put one over on HH.

Two weeks went by, and Fen's secret remained safe. Brat had returned from Hitty's and was hard at work mapping in the science lab and working with Luc in the office.

When time permitted, he read a history on the exile of the Netherworld Ruler and his band of followers. Heroic ploys of HH. *No history in this book,* Brat said to himself.

Then one night, a high-ranking military officer strode into the office and asked for Fen. He was tall, dressed in black, and similar to HH in appearance. The grim expression on his stern face seemed to fill the room with a cold blast of air, and for a moment, Brat shivered. *A certified heroic confederate of HH,* he thought.

After the visit, Fen wore an air of desperation. His temper frayed easily, and Luc bore the brunt of his outbursts. Towards the end of the third week, Fen came into the office looking worn and haggard. He went into his inner office and banged the door shut. An hour later, he came out and said, "Bo, you're finding astral paths. Can you find a lost Daggie?"

"Never tried it, boss," Brat replied. "Who is it you're trying to trace?"

"A Daggie went missing a few weeks ago and my agents haven't located him. It's critical that he be found."

"It will take me a few nights to search Dluse. I may have to be out of the office occasionally. In what region did he live?"

"He's from Nofer a town in Daganland. He was a student who pulled a stunt and ran away while he was serving a sentence at The Works. HH intends to make him his assistant."

Brat, speechless for a moment, managed to say, "A Daggie, HH's assistant?"

"HH likes the Daggie and what HH likes he gets. Find him for me, and be quick about it."

"I'll start tonight. Where can I get a map of Dluse?"

"Luc, find him a map," Fen said, and went back to his office.

Luc dug in his desk drawer and handed Brat a map. He took it and looked at the spot where Daganland intersected the human world. He concentrated for the next two days on learning the astral pathways from Nofer to Lydo. *I'm ousting this assistant thing,* Brat thought as he worked with a resolute aim in mind.

HH sent Fen to Nofer to interrogate his agents on their search and to explore any overlooked avenues. When Fen found his security forces in the pub, he was furious and packed them off to Synlan. "I'll deal with the lot of you when I get back," he roared.

At The Works, he questioned Faln, who trembling in fear, said, "You want to know where Brat went? If I knew your agents would have spared their blows to my head."

At last, in anger and frustration, Fen said, "Do you know where the Daggie came from?"

"I do not. The Intake Division has that information."

Fen went off fuming and raging to question the intake staff. They denied any knowledge of Brat's former life, but gave him the file on Brat's testing and his assignment to the educational department.

"You are more inept than the security forces," Fen barked. He looked closely at Brat's score on the test and a vague idea began forming in his mind. "I'll take this file with me," he said.

When he arrived home, he went to his office, called Luc to come in, and said to him, "Get in touch with Lexter's intake department, and request their records on a nineteen year old named Brat. Ask them for all the records dating back a year."

Luc sent the request off to Lexter on the office Trans com that was off limits to everyone except Luc and Fen.

The luxuries of Synlan, Brat thought as he watched Luc send the request.

Fen stepped to the door of his office and asked Brat to come in.

A sense of something wrong came over him when he saw Fen's face. He grinned at Brat and said, "Made any headway with tracing the missing Daggie?"

"I'm hot on his trail,' Brat replied. " A couple of days will do it."

"Excellent," Fen replied and dismissed him.

Wheeling Home

16

Brat stayed three hours in the lab searching for the best possible route from Nofer to Lydo. *No time to lose*, he thought. *When Fen grins, someone is in for it.* He finally found the most likely path and mapped it. *Eight hours to get there and a hot pursuit by Fen when I'm missed.*

The next night at the lab, he asked the old professor for permission to view the aerial capsules. The hangars were close by and Brat went alone to view them. He saw a sign above the door of the nearest one; 'Reserved for Dignitaries.' Assorted capsules were suspended along the walls according to their use.

One, a silver metallic color, designed for both ground transport and space voyages, caught his eye. It was reserved solely for the Head Honcho. *The right size for us,* he thought and checked the inner mechanisms.

An hour passed while Brat verified the capsule's readiness for travel. When he placed his hands on the buttons to stop and start the craft a sense of familiarity came to him. Satisfied he went back to the lab, thanked the old professor, and continued working on the astral pathways.

Professor Mikol and Commander Raal of the Inter-galactic military forces of Iru viewed Brat's actions in the Hangar and deduced his plans. "He's going to do a runner with the three Daggies," Professor Mikol said. "HH will be enraged and set off in pursuit when Brat goes missing. I feel responsible for him."

"You weren't alone in approving his visit to Dluse," Commander Raal said. "We didn't quite understand the remarkable student we sent into a risky setting. We'll put the forces on high alert and send two warriors to escort him home if the Synlan forces prove dangerous."

The Commander went to his office and spoke to his aides who then put the alert system in place. The two warriors, Mel and Cal, were notified of an emergency that required their immediate presence. An expert in universal voice technics threw a switch, which connected to Nofer and Synlan. It was now a wait for developing events.

When the message from the Lexter intake department came in next night, an excited Luc took it to Fen. "No intake for a Brat in our system. The files for the past three years were searched without results," the memo stated.

Fen rubbed his head and ordered Luc to remain silent about the message. Brat took in the reactions of Luc and Fen to the message and a sense of urgency flowed over him. *A Gulag message for someone and the someone may be me,* he thought.

Fen remained in his office with the door closed during the early night hours. He knew without doubt that his assistant was Brat. If HH knew the Daggie had managed to join his security force he, Fen, would be fired. The Daggie might even be put in charge of the security forces. He must get rid of him at once to keep HH from finding out.

The plan settled, Fen left the office with Luc. "This is what you are to do," Fen said, "Take Bo to security head-quarters on some pretext tonight. My personal guards will arrest him and take him down to the seventh floor. The Daggie will stay lost, and HH will never know the dif-ference."

Fen forgot that loyalty was a word without meaning in Synlan.

Brat finished his mapping, rid his desk of any in-formation that might give clues to his destination, and left for the lab. The old professor was in the auditorium giv-ing a lecture to his astronomy students. Brat went to the Aerial Hangar and soon had the capsule on the launching pad. He climbed in and pushed the button for departure.

The machine ascended silently and five minutes later, he set down behind Hitty's building.

Two hours head start, maybe more, and perhaps another hour before the Aerial Hangar is checked, he thought as he knocked on Hitty's door. He then ran from the building and was ready for takeoff when Hitty and the twins scurried into the capsule. "No time for talking," he said, "I'm fleeing to Lydo. Your choice to stay or go."

"We're going with you, Brat," Hitty said. "So go." Brat tapped a button and the craft lifted into the air. "We'll enter the aerial path to Lydo in one minute or less. I removed any traces of where we're going, but Fen will begin to suspect before the night is over."

"The worst that can happen is the Gulag," Hitty said. "They can't kill us."

"They can be mean," Luna said and began to cry.

"Dry your tears Sis," Wim said. "No use to spill tears on imaginary things."

Brat said, "Brace yourselves. We're entering the star trail to Lydo, a shortcut I discovered this week."

Suddenly a strong wind seemed to envelope the capsule, and they felt a heavy pressure on their bodies. Then the pressure eased, and the noiseless capsule glided through the pocket of space at a limitless speed.

"The controls are set on automatic to reach the Lydo city of Iru in eight hours," Brat said. "We have two or three hours before Fen discovers I'm missing."

"Why go to Lydo, Brat?" Hitty said.

"Tell us, Brat," Wim said.

"Dluse is monitored by Lydo agents. I read the files. Fen put me to work to find hidden space routes so his agents could destroy their system. I figured if HH raged against Lydo, it had to be a better place than Synlan."

"Did you discover any hidden routes to Lydo, Brat?" Hitty asked.

"No, Hitty. This route is the closest I got to one. It was used less than six months ago by someone but not by the agents of HH. My calculations led me to the aerial imprints within the loops we're traveling through."

"What if Fen's security forces catch up with us, Brat? What then?" Wim said.

"We'll be in Lydo's aerial space in six hours. We'll try to hang on and hope our craft is faster than Fen's military craft."

In Iru, Professor Mikol and Commander Raal were mesmerized by the sheer audacity of Brad and the three Daggies. A report on Fen's plan to send Brad to the Gulag came in. "It may give Brad more time. Fear of HH will delay the news of Brad's escape if Luc doesn't rat on Fen," Professor Mikol said.

"We'll wait for developments. Our orders are to avoid conflict with the Synlanese if at all possible," Commander Raal said. "If Brat is pursued, perhaps we can scare off his pursuers without a skirmish."

"Is the military on standby?"

"The aerial force was alerted hours ago. Mel and Cal are in flight and due to arrive any minute. Their help will be invaluable if conflict arises," Commander Raal replied.

Fen's plans for Brat were going awry. Luc bypassed Building G and the lab. Instead, he went straight to the palace and asked to see HH. "He's in a meeting and isn't free at present," an aide said. "Can I assist you?"

"I'll wait until he's free, and no you can't assist me," Luc said. Thirty minutes later the aide came in. "He'll see you now." He led Luc through a corridor and knocked on a door. When a voice said, "Come in," the aide scooted away. Luc went in, looked at the ruthless face of HH, and lost his speech for a minute.

"What do you want? Did Fen send you? Speak up."

"N-no, Fen didn't send me," Luc stuttered. "I came to tell you the Daggie has been found."

"Where is he? Bring him to me. How come Fen didn't tell me?"

Luc, oozing fear from every pore, told him how Brat had come to Synlan as a security recruit and was working as Fen's assistant under an assumed name. HH's face grew black and thunderous as the whole story unfolded. "Where is Fen? No, hold on. Don't bother with him. Let him burrow deeper into his deceit. Go bring the Daggie to me. He's smarter that all of you put together."

Luc went to Brat's lodgings and then to the lab. The old professor said it was Bo's half night off. By the time, Luc checked the Mess Hall and went back to Brat's lodgings, he was becoming panicky. He lingered for an hour before reluctantly trudging back to the palace.

When Luc confessed he could not find Brat, HH's face grew even blacker and he roared, "Fen will pay for this. The Daggie found him out and ran again. Get the security forces out looking for him. He couldn't have gotten far."

Every corner of the city was searched in the next hour without result. Two hours passed, and then HH said, "He went to Nofer, the only possible place. Get my Air V ready, Luc. You and I are going to Daganland."

"Hold Fen at security headquarters," HH snapped to an aide.

Luc had the aide call the porter of the Aerial Hangar while he went to do a preliminary inspection of the Air V. The bewildered porter met him at the door, gesturing towards the empty space where the Air V usually hung. Luc was terrified of having to tell HH. When he did, the roars threatened mayhem to all. He sent Luc back to the Aerial Hangar to prepare another Air V. "The fastest one I have," he ordered.

They arrived in Nofer five minutes later and went to Hitty's apartment. The apartment was empty. Luc questioned the building's residents, but they knew nothing. Daganland's security agents were called in to search.

The only information gained in an hours search was the fact of two missing students. "Fen is responsible for this mess," HH fumed. "I'll sack every last one of my security agents. Luc, the Daggie worked with you in the office. What did he do?"

"He's a genius in astronomical calculations. We had him looking for hidden routes to Lydo."

"You and Fen are dummies. Don't you see what happened? He has taken off to Lydo with the three other Daggies. Fen scared him, so he's running. Farther this time. The brainy types are sensitive. Wait 'til I get my hands on Fen."

On the way back to the palace, HH said, "We're going after him. If the three Daggies are with him, he followed an aerial path close to Nofer. Stop by the lab."

Luc parked the Air V at the Hangar, and they went into the lab. When the old commander came in, Luc said, "Have no fear." He gestured to HH who stood behind Luc with his hooded eyes on both of them. "We're here to ask your help in finding an aerial route from Nofer to Lydo."

The old commander said, "Eh, Bo showed me a partial calculation on a route the other night. It may not be the one, but I will try to finish it, eh?" He went to his desk, took some papers from his drawer and began to calculate. He finished in twenty minutes and gave the sheet to Luc. "Eh...it's not a route we use, but Bo may have taken it to avoid our monitors, eh."

"We have nothing else to go on. It will do," HH said. "Commander, program the route into my Aerial V and then call five military aces to follow us."

HH said as he and Luc began the hunt with the military craft. "We have to go full throttle. I'm not losing my Daggies to Lydo, those spying scoundrels. They are hours ahead of us, but this craft is faster than the one Brat took."

Commander Raal and Professor Mikol met with Mel and Cal who had arrived and considered the circumstances. Brought up to date on Brad's position, they then discussed the best approach. The two warriors would attempt to get in between the crafts of Brad and HH, and his military forces. Was it possible to find a parallel route to draw the forces away from Brad?"

Professor Mikol turned to commander Raal. "Do we have a shorter route?"

"If we don't, it's possible to create one."

"What about it, Mel?" The commander asked.

"We can use the interlinking route Cal and I traveled when we were sent to cheer a human boy who is now secure in our Supreme Lord's service."

"And now Brad must gain the security of home," Cal said. "We can do it. The routes connect about two hours from here."

"You two go ahead, and we will follow," Commander Raal said. "Brad will be almost three hours ahead of HH."

Mel and Cal were in a flight path light years away from the military forces of HH. The monitor showed the distance narrowing between Brad and HH as the two warriors entered their space vehicle and departed.

"Time for us to bring our youngster home," Professor Mikol said. "The visit to Dluse has given him enough excitement for a while."

"Don't forget us," Commander Raal said. They entered the military space capsule with two flight engineers and traced their way to Brat among the stars.

Brat saw on the flight VDU, the pursuing craft of HH and behind him his military forces. They were distant specks but coming on at full speed. Hitty gazed at the specks and said, "Does this thing go faster, Brat?"

"We're at the upper speed, Hitty. One more hour to reach the Lydo aerial zone."

Luna wrung her hands and said, "Faster, Brat, faster. The meanies will get us."

Hitty looked closely at the VDU and said, "What are those two dots high on the right corner of this thing."

"Even as they looked the dots grew larger and moved between Brat and their pursuers. "Multiple attackers on two fronts?" Brat said. "We won't be beaten without a fight." He pushed a button on the flight controls and the capsule increased its speed.

"Our flight path crosses another route along here somewhere, but I didn't have time to explore it," Brat said.

They gazed intently as the dots increased in size. Then Brat noticed a difference in the two capsules that moved between them and the pursuing craft. Light radiated in flowing waves from them and engulfed the pursuing craft.

"Friends perhaps," Brat said. "We can hope it is, anyhow."

The pursuing craft attempted to go around the two capsules. The light stopped it repeatedly. Five more pursuing capsules hove into view and flares of red appeared in the sky.

At the border of Lydo's airspace, the pursuers turned and began a retreat. The two crafts moved to the front of Brat's capsule and a third craft joined them.

A voice crackled from the VDU and made everyone jump. "Enemy has left. Follow us to Iru."

All aboard expelled their breath in a big whoosh. "The air from our breath could propel us to Iru," Wim said.

"Brat, what if we don't look like the beings of Iru?" Hitty said.

"We won't let looks faze us, Hitty, or other obstacles that may await us."

"We won't, Luna said, and squeezed the hand she had held in a firm grip since leaving Nofer.

"In that case, Luna," Hitty said, "would you permit me to liberate the hand you've squeezed to a pulp."

"I'm hungry," Wim said. "What if Iru food is different than ours?"

"We'll eat whatever is offered," Brat said.

"Horror of horrors, what if they don't need to eat," Hitty said.

"That's enough from you two," Brat said. "Fine time to go wobbly."

Quietness prevailed until the VDU vibrated and a clear voice said, "Prepare for landing."

"First phase ended," Brat said. "To the second, gang." He pushed a button and the capsule began descending. Professor Mikol and Commander Raal met them at the aerial dock.

Brat, Hitty and the twins stared at the beings standing in front of them. Their form resembled the humans, but theirs was far more radiant as if from the glow of a light within. Professor Mikol was dark haired and dressed in a pair of loose trousers beneath a light green tunic with an emerald green sash at the waist. Sturdy brown sandals were laced to his ankles. Commander Raal was dressed in a blue uniform and black boots that encased his feet and legs to the knees. His cap covered curly brown hair. Both were about six feet tall.

"Are we to stand here staring at each other for the next hour, or would you prefer to go to the Lab?" Professor Mikol said in the dialect of Dluse. He and commander Raal introduced themselves.

Brat said, "Thanks for the rescue. We were in a spot of trouble."

"Only a spot, Brad. Your flight has been monitored since leaving Nofer." commander Raal said.

"Welcome to our city, Hitty, Luna, and Wim. The census trackers traced your names from the Dluse files." Professor Mikol said.

At the lab, they were shown to a conference room where they were given food and drink. "Two questions decided, Hitty," Brat said. "Food and casings, or bodies as the humans term them. These beings resemble the ones in my dreams. As you said, the dream will bring an answer."

"What dreams?" Luna asked.

"Doesn't matter, Luna. A tale for another day."

"The food gets an approval," Wim said.

"I suspect it's Daggie food," Hitty said.

An hour later Professor Mikol came in and asked to see Hitty, Wim and Luna alone.

Brat was taken to another room. "I'm used to hither and thither goings," he said to the white coated lab attendant.

"Hither and thither will be brief, Brad. In a trice," she said, smiling at him.

Professor Mikol looked at Hitty and the twins and said, "If your choice is to remain with us, there are options I want to present to each of you."

Hitty interrupted him, "No choice for me. Brat's home is my home."

"And ours," Wim said.

"Then, I will tell you, Brad's home is here in Iru. He's a student at the astronomy institute and elected to take a field trip to Dluse for his behavioral studies."

"Sounds like my Brat, but how come we look the same if his home is here?" Hitty said.

"We have variant convertors called M&M's that are used to alter a being's outer shape. Before he went to Nofer Brad completed the process with memory erasure."

"So that's why he couldn't remember where he came from," Hitty said.

"The imprint remained, however, and brought him home," Professor Mikol said. "You have memories of your origin, Hitty?"

"I haven't a clue, Professor. A white house is the only item that popped into my mind when Brat and I discussed it."

"Luna, Wim, do you have memories of your origin?"

"As we explained to Brat, Professor. Our memories are dim. We have a fleeting memory of a thunderous crash before we woke up in Daganland." Wim replied."

"Then, it's a simple solution. We can recover your memories and body of your prior life, or we can arrange for you to resemble us in form. It is your decision."

"When Brat comes to us in his Iru form, we'll give you an answer, Professor Mikol," Hitty replied.

"A good decision, Hitty. You will see him inside two hours."

"I want to look like, Brat," Luna said when the Professor had withdrawn.

"Think I'll have a nap," Hitty said, "while we wait."

The three crossed to cots against the wall and lay down. Two hours later, they were awakened by the voice of a tall young male, "Wake up, it's me, Brat." He was standing near their cots dressed in an ivory tunic and loose pants with a pale green sash encircling his waist. On his feet were golden sandals of an unknown fabric. Each pair of eyes opened and rounded to a gaze of wonder.

Hitty shook her head from side to side and then said, "Brat? Is that you, Brat? Your voice is the same. You're a mite taller with flaxen hair that frames a rosy face. But the familiar light of your old teasing manner is in those new blue eyes."

"You haven't lost your wit, Hitty," Brad said.

The twins jumped up from their cots and clung to his hands. "I want to look like Brat," Luna repeated.

"No, Luna, your appearance will be a unique feminine self," Brad replied.

"We measure time by light years in Iru, Wim. You will remain seventeen. You and Luna will continue your studies in the department of administration near my campus."

"My dearest, Hitty. Will you agree to be my Iru Advisor? You will have your own white house, and the twins and I will drop in for chats and clamor for a feeding."

"Our Advisor, too, Hitty." Luna said.

"You're going to fast for me. Be quiet, and let me think," Hitty said.

"Will a light year do, Hitty?"

"Keep still a minute, Brat, or is it Brad?"

"I began as Brat and Brat I will remain to my three friends."

"Well, I didn't come all this way to change my occupation. You're my charge whether in Nofer or Iru. In your rephrased words to me; we four will toddle down the light years together."

"A toddlin' we will go, Hitty. Let us now amble to the Chamber of Changes. After you have slipped into your new outer garbs with a time-out for admiration, an Iru snack is on order.

"We'll sit by the river and reflect on the vagaries of life and watch the dappled sunlight upon the water. Then, we'll wend our way home to an Iru feast prepared by Professor Mikol. Three other guests will join us, Mel and Cal, who led us safely here, and Commander Raal."

"Home? Where is home, Brat?" Luna asked.

"Patience, Luna. First, a viewing is scheduled for a white house. From there, we'll proceed to an apartment complex where my digs are located. Your terraced flat on the second floor is waiting for occupancy. A tad more room than our staclets."

"Oh joy," Luna said. She reached for Wim's hand and beamed at Hitty.

"This takes some getting used to, Brat," Hitty said. "I have to wrap my head around these things."

"Wrap to your heart's content, Hitty," Brad replied. "In the meantime, the wizards of M&M are in the Chamber. Come, let's join them and chuck the nightlife. Add the day life to your wraps."

Two hours later three newly minted Lydians emerged to begin a new life with Brad in the city of Iru.

Character names

Beterbe—Better be
Bogis — Bogus
Buetee—Beauty
Cunin—Cunning
Cheter—Cheater
Dogmihyde—Dog my hide
Faln—Fallen
Husslm—Hustle them
Kruknsak—Crook and sac
Letcher—Lecher
Luc Luke
Lydo-Lee doe
Luter—Looter
Polwin—Poll win
Seeznsken—Seize and skin
Selnby—Sell and buy
Spadd—Spade
Swinne—Swine
Takachek —Take a check
Weezl — Weasel
Staclet—stack let(Unit of residence)

About The Author

Nancy Janes lives in the Blue Ridge Mountains of North Carolina with her husband, Richard. She writes Sc/fic/ fantasy and short stories in the Americana vein.

The present book is loosely based on a previous book The Boy Who Walked A Way. Both are stories of the land of Light and The land of Darkness.

http://www.amazon.com/dp/B00V97LGTC

Reader,

If you have enjoyed this book, please take a few minutes to post a review on Amazon. It will help greatly to expand the message to others.
http://www.amazon.com/dp/B00V97LGTC

I will be most grateful for your help.

Nancy Janes

www.ingramcontent.com/pod-product-compliance
Lightning Source LLC
Chambersburg PA
CBHW060139130626
46556CB00006B/2409